Mystery at the Asylum

Miss Hayward and the Detective series

By Helen Goltz

Atlas Productions

For Jane Wilson
Thank you, dear Jane.

With a glance to the sky – the bluest of skies – Hilda Rodgers felt a rush of excitement. She was convinced it was time. Her wings were ready, flight would be welcomed.

The journey felt like it had been a long one, years of struggle, but now she was at peace, even euphoric at the idea of her release to the wind.

Hilda lifted her skirts a little to avoid tripping while looking skyward. She moved along with the sweep of ladies and gentlemen walking along the footpath of the Victoria Bridge with its lacework parapet and extensive view of the river on both sides.

Finding the middle, she stopped, slightly breathless, to admire the view with the handful of couples doing the same as they promenaded. It is what they had come for on this fine winter afternoon.

But Hilda lingered, not encouraging an audience to her flight. It was her first, after all, and it was fair to say she was a little nervous.

Assured now of no one immediately around her, Hilda leaned over the railing, extended her arms and with a small jump, pushed her weight forward and fell.

Around her, for just a few seconds she registered screams, but then the scream came from within her. There was no flight, no wings, she was flailing.

Chapter 1

Matilda Hayward scanned the pages of the daily newspaper as she ate her breakfast of toast and jam with tea. Mr Hayward, her father, sat nearby, reading the other half of the paper and sharing stories with Matilda, as interest prevailed. Upon finishing, they swapped pages; the routine was well-established.

'Oh goodness, there's been another break-in and not too far from our abode. I hope our excellent police service is onto it,' Mr Hayward said with a glance at Matilda and a smile. Both parties knew the very clever detective courting Matilda would not be wasted on a routine break and enter.

'I am sure they will apprehend the desperados in no time, Pa,' she agreed with a grin. 'Did you see your stock is up?'

'Indeed. Might be time to sell.'

They returned to their reading. Earlier this morning they had seen Elijah – now Dr Elijah Hayward and the first doctor in the family – off to his new posting at an asylum hospital and Matilda was keen to visit with him. Mrs Dora Lawson, her editor at the *Women's Journal* where Matilda was gainfully employed, had said Matilda's writing would benefit from understanding more about life, from empathy gained with experience. She told Matilda it "rounds off our character and adds depth to our work, but there is nothing like having personal life experience. Often that comes with age." That was all well and good, but Matilda didn't have the benefit of age on her side at 22, and while she had grown up without a mother, Matilda could not claim that as a hardship when she barely remembered her. She had been cocooned in the love of her father, four brothers, Aunt Audrey, housekeeper Harriet, cook Mary, and childhood friend, Thomas Ashdown, who had since become much more than a friend. Matilda sighed.

'What is it, my dear?' her father asked.

'I need to experience more of life, Pa,' Matilda said.

'Right this minute?' he teased, and she chuckled.

'Yes, Pa, immediately, there is no time to spare,' she said and gave him a wry look. 'Mrs Lawson said more life experience would benefit my writing.'

'Ah, there is truth in that, and plenty of life to observe in the every day.' Her father studied her and then reached for her hand, giving it a squeeze. They returned to their newspapers.

'Goodness, look at this!' Matilda pointed to a minor story with a headline larger than the accompanying text. 'Woman jumps from Victoria Bridge.'

'That's the second death there in less than a month,' Mr Hayward said. 'What does it say?'

'Very little. Perhaps the story arrived on deadline,'

Matilda said, now familiar with print press deadlines since having started in the industry. 'It reads:

'Mrs Hilda Agnes Rodgers, 44, of Sussex Street, West End, received injuries from which she died shortly afterwards in the General Hospital. Mrs Rodgers jumped from the Victoria Bridge. This was the second fatal fall from the bridge within a few weeks. Hundreds of persons witnessed today's tragedy. Making a tremendous splash, a small schooner nearby was able to locate Mrs Rodgers and went to her immediate rescue. Police are investigating.'

'Terrible,' Mr Hayward said.

The bell on the front door rang and Matilda and Mr Hayward listened as Harriet opened the door and greeted the guest. They exchanged looks as they heard the foot treads heading their way – visitors at breakfast were rare and they hoped bad news was not forthwith. Harriet put their minds at ease as she appeared relaxed in the dining room doorway.

'Thomas has arrived, and yes, I told him he does not need to be announced,' she said with a smile as Matilda beamed.

'Come on in, Thomas,' Mr Hayward called, and Thomas appeared beside Harriet.

'Forgive the early intrusion, hence I thought it best not to barge in just in case you were not dressed for company,' Thomas said and gave Mr Hayward and his beloved Matilda a small bow.

'Not at all, come, join us, we are always dressed for family,' Mr Hayward said, and Matilda began to rise.

'Please do not disturb yourself,' he told her, holding her gaze longer than that of Mr Hayward. He accepted the invitation and sat opposite Matilda and beside Mr Hayward as Harriet bought him a cup of tea. He thanked her and declined the offer of breakfast.

'I was in the area on a case and thought perhaps I could accompany you to the *Women's Journal* if you were heading that way this morning,' he said.

'That would be wonderful.' Matilda beamed. 'I shall go and prepare.'

'There is no hurry,' Thomas said, but Matilda knew he would be in a hurry. He always was when it came to work.

'I forget since taking retirement that it is not an early hour for the working man,' Mr Hayward said.

'Do you miss practising the law?' Thomas asked of Mr Hayward's legal career.

'I can honestly say that I don't. And I am surprised by that,' Mr Hayward said with a smile.

'What are you working on, Thomas?' Matilda asked enthusiastically. She read his expression. 'Not for publication, of course.'

Mr Hayward chuckled.

Thomas looked uncomfortable. 'It's a delicate matter,' he said, with a glance at Mr Hayward.

'Thomas is right, not a breakfast conversation,' Mr Hayward said, picking up on Thomas's discomfort.

'I shall go and get ready then,' Matilda said. Both

gentlemen half-rose from their chairs as she stood and slid her section of the paper over to Thomas, tapping on the story of the lady falling to her death.

'I'm sure I shall get it out of you on the way, Thomas,' she teased and turned to her father. 'I shall tell you later, Pa.'

Mr Hayward laughed and shook his head. Thomas made a harrumph sound and turned to Mr Hayward. 'I suspect she will,' he said.

Mr Hayward chuckled. 'Most likely, Thom,' he said with affection. 'None of us can keep any secrets from Matilda, can we, dear? Perhaps she should have been an investigator.'

She stopped in the doorway long enough to hear Thomas mutter, 'Heaven help me,' and to give him an eye roll that earned Thomas another chuckle from his potential father-in-law.

Chapter 2

The hansom cab stopped outside the imposing gates of the Asylum for the Insane at Wacol, Brisbane. Dr Elijah Hayward glanced out before alighting.

'You sure this is the place you were after, sir?' the driver asked, leaning down to speak with his passenger, who appeared to be too sane to be a resident, and too well-dressed to be visiting.

'This is the place,' Elijah said and stepped down.

'Don't think I can wait around, sorry,' the driver said nervously.

'No need to,' Elijah assured him. He thanked the driver and paid him for the journey. The driver needed no encouragement to turn around and depart as quickly as he arrived. Elijah smiled; the reaction was expected.

He turned and entered through the asylum gates. Elijah knew he had drawn the short straw being sent to tend to the insane, but secretly, he was excited. As a newly qualified doctor, the more experience he gained in the most diverse places, the better. Besides, he had always wanted to help those truly in need rather than those who could afford consultation over the most minor issues – like Miss Lily Chappell, whose regular appointments were becoming more like courting than needing medical attention. He had studied for too long and too hard at a great cost to his Aunt Audrey – Mrs Samuel Bloomfield – to be on hand to the fairer sex and their games. Some doctors attended to women's nerves; he was not one of them.

He suspected he would not have to worry about that in his new position. Elijah had studied the report: just over 350 male patients and 200 females, and the senior doctor, Stephen O'Shea, had allocated Elijah to the women's asylum. With so many female patients, he'd barely have time to breathe. Pleasing to note were the 130 of those assigned to useful work, for Elijah believed being occupied in mind and body cured many illnesses.

He took a deep breath; the asylum was a forbidding building, to say the least. Elijah had warned his sister, Matilda, that it was so, but she was still keen to join him on one of his rostered shifts and research the conditions of ladies locked up for the *Women's Journal*, her place of employment. He was one year her senior, and they had not always seen eye to eye being so close in age, but now, as adults, they had become closer.

Elijah entered the gates, walked the path up the drive, and took the stairs to the main building. With a deep breath, he pushed open the large timber and iron door. The smell of antiseptic hit his senses; at least it smelled clean, he thought.

Elijah had only taken a few steps into the large reception area before an imposing matron greeted him. He had met a few in the years he had studied in hospitals in Sydney and found their bark and their bluff worse than their bite.

'Visiting hours have not started yet, I'm afraid,' the stout nurse said to him. She walked around from behind the desk as if to shoo him out. Elijah noted the matron had the misfortune of being the same shape from the shoulders down, a portly woman but well presented.

'Visiting hours are not a deterrent,' he said with a smile. 'I'm Dr Elijah Hayward. I'm here to take up a posting and meet—'

'Me!'

Elijah turned at hearing the voice behind him.

'Thank you, Matron Gormley, I'll take care of the good doctor.' An energetic and tall man appeared beside him, offering his hand. In his thirties, by appearances, with thinning hair in keeping with his thin body, his energy added to his charisma.

'Dr Stephen O'Shea at your service,' he said with a small bow, 'and you must be my new assistant.'

The men shook and Elijah introduced himself, meeting Matron Gormley formally at the same time.

'Dr Hayward will assist me with the management of the female ward,' Dr O'Shea told the matron; 'and Dr Victor McQuade will continue to assist me in the male ward.'

'Right you are then, Doctor,' she said and bustled back behind the desk. 'No need to sign in then, Dr Hayward.'

Dr O'Shea turned to Elijah. 'You'll meet Victor tomorrow

morning. We convene here at eight o'clock, then if there are no issues to share and discuss, Victor and I will do our rounds of the male wards which takes about two hours, then I'll seek you out and we'll do the rounds of the female wards. I've got him in the wards now, starting without me as I was expecting your arrival this morning.'

'I understand,' Elijah said, 'so in the morning before the rounds, I tend patients, check medications, and so forth as required?'

'Exactly, you've obviously done this in your local hospital rounds?'

'A few times,' Elijah agreed with a grin.

'Then let me give you the tour and introduce you to your patients – those who require little care, the colourful characters, and our more demanding patients,' he said with a glance to Matron Gormley, who sighed on cue.

A shrill scream came from one wing. The doctor and matron ignored as if it was a common occurrence; perhaps it was. Dr O'Shea headed off at a speed that only someone with legs of his length could reach, and Elijah hurried to keep up with him.

'I assure you, every female in residence who is declared insane will do her best to tell you she is not, in fact, insane, and those who are not declared insane invariably are,' Dr O'Shea said.

'So, they are all insane?' Elijah asked, confused.

'Let's just say it's a rare bird that isn't,' Dr O'Shea said with a wink.

Chapter 3

Matilda admired her beau as he pressed his lips to her hand. It still surprised her seeing the handsome Thomas Ashdown, her childhood friend, now taking the role of her suitor. Apparently, she was the only one surprised, according to her family.

'This is a lovely surprise, Thomas,' she said. 'I get to see you, and I get a hansom ride to work instead of the omnibus.'

'Well, I was heading right past the office of the *Women's Journal,* so it seemed too good an opportunity,' he said.

They made a handsome couple – the tall fair-headed detective dressed in a dark suit and well-groomed, and the young lady in a fitted red suit, with the collar of her crisp white blouse peeking out of her jacket, a straw hat and black ribbon perched on her golden hair.

'You look particularly lovely today. Have you missed me?' he asked.

'Since yesterday's lunch?' she asked and then on seeing his expression added, 'Of course, I've thought of nothing but you.'

Thomas narrowed his eyes, and she laughed.

'I always miss you when you leave, and worry about you,' she assured him. 'But at least seeing you for Sunday lunch, I get a dose of you to last a short while.'

'Like medicine,' he said wryly.

'The good tasting medicine,' she declared. 'Have you missed me?'

'Of course. I hope that one day soon we don't have to say goodbye to each other at the end of the day.'

Matilda reddened slightly at his implication. 'I know what police work hours are like, so I suspect I will be home a lot more than you. So what case are you on your way to now?' She deftly changed the subject.

Thomas cleared his throat. 'The death of a woman in her late thirties.'

'Ah-ha, it is the bridge fall, isn't it?' she asked, her eyes widened with interest.

Thomas nodded. 'Yes, the one you saw in the newspaper.'

'How positively awful.' Matilda shuddered.

'Indeed.'

'She must have been so frightened while falling.' Matilda studied Thomas. 'So, it wasn't an accidental fall then if you are investigating it. Was it murder or—'

'I can't answer your questions,' he cut her off, and seeing her stubborn expression added, 'I don't know myself yet. The coroner has asked to see me. Harry is meeting me there, and then I'll know more.'

She nodded, satisfied with the answer.

'And we are here,' he said, as the hansom came to a stop outside Matilda's place of employment. 'Allow me to help you out,' he offered, and then gave her a grin, expecting her challenge. She had given Thomas a run for his money many a time as younger competitors in sport and play, but now society dictated that Matilda must wear restrictive skirts and appear the lady.

'Helpless as I am, I willingly accept your assistance,' she answered.

'Is that so? There's a first for everything.' He laughed, surprised, and stepping down, offered his hand, which Matilda accepted as she alighted.

'Why?' he then asked, suspicious.

'I am keen to show you off to any of the ladies of the *Women's Journal* who might glance out or pass.' She noted the look of delight on his face.

He bade her farewell and hurried back into the cab, giving the driver the address. Matilda watched him depart, content she had compensated for not swooning enough earlier. It was challenging, she conceded, expressing romantic thoughts to a man who had grown up as a brother to her. But all that was changing.

*****

A dead body on a slab was no surprise to the two detectives, but nevertheless, Thomas was always relieved it wasn't him there being inspected by the coroner, Dr Patrick Nevins, whose reputation as one of the best preceded him. Today's deceased, a middle-aged woman nearing forty, rested face down. Dr Nevins pulled back the sheet to waist level.

'Good grief,' Detective Harry Dart said on seeing her exposed back.

It amazed Thomas that his mature partner was shocked by anything after all his years of duty. He wasn't looking forward to the day when Harry retired; it was a few years away yet. They were well partnered, and Harry mentored him without the insecurity of having a young gun partner with the best success rate for solving crime in the state.

'I'm gathering that scarring and bruising did not come about from the fall?' Thomas asked.

'Correct,' Dr Nevins said and sighed. 'She had been mistreated, which may explain why she took her own life in such a brutal fashion, if she did,' he added.

'Our witness statements all claim she fell, and no one was seen near enough to have pushed her,' Thomas said. 'Perhaps that was an easy way out for her compared to what she was going through somewhere else.'

'Yes,' Dr Nevins agreed. He took his steel-rimmed glasses off and, fishing a small handkerchief from his pocket, cleaned them as he spoke to the two detectives. 'Death was as the result of the fall and her wounds were consistent with impact. It surprised me she didn't die immediately, but the poor woman lingered long enough to give hope to a loved one,' he said, pushing his glasses back on and pocketing the material. 'However, these wounds tell a different story.'

'There's old and new?' Harry asked.

'Yes,' Dr Nevins said. 'Some bruises are fresh, but many of the scars are quite old.'

'How old?' Thomas asked.

The coroner gave a small shrug. 'Years, I'd say, but adult years, not childhood. Some of her wounds are consistent with a beating from a cane, some with a whip – a short whip.'

Thomas ground his teeth, an action he did when frustrated. He could never imagine raising a hand to Matilda. What sort of man feels empowered by punishing a woman?

'But there are a few wounds that may interest you both.' The coroner turned the body over to reveal some markings on the neck. 'I would say a fist has administered these wounds.' He indicated some fresh bruising and cuts, then lifted the right hand of the body to show the two men the bruised and red wrist. 'This is a restraint mark; it is likely from a powerful hand that has held the deceased, see the finger mark bruising around her wrist?'

Thomas turned to Harry. 'Maybe from someone who tried to drag her up on the bridge or flung her off it.'

'Or tried to restrain and pull her back,' Harry suggested, offering another perspective.

'Thanks, Patrick, we'll leave you with the dead then,' Thomas said and held the door open for Harry, who gave a wave of thanks to Dr Nevins.

'Let's meet the family,' Harry suggested.

Chapter 4

The staff meeting at the *Women's Journal* was a much-anticipated event. Matilda loved being among the women of all ages with varied skills – writers, illustrators, editors, and she was particularly in awe of the editor, Mrs Dora Lawson. She took her seat next to fellow writer and friend, Alice Doran, and listened to the discussion at hand before Mrs Lawson called the meeting to order. Today, it was all about the lady who fell to her death, and it appeared the lady and her situation were known to several of the staff.

Mrs Lawson sat at the head of the table next to her deputy editor, Betty Purcell, and greeted the group. A handsome woman in her mature years with white hair pinned neatly atop, Mrs Lawson was not one to start a meeting late.

'A sad state of affairs indeed,' she said, summing up what everyone had been talking about. 'Betty and I know a little about the background of the poor lady in question. She was quite an amazing lady, a true crusader for women's rights.'

Betty nodded, and a few gasps could be heard around the table.

'Then why would she jump, Mrs Lawson? Do you think she was pushed?' Georgina Urry, one of the journal's illustrators, asked.

Matilda like Georgina because of her frankness. She would make a good journalist, as she was never afraid to say what she thought and was always most direct. Her imposing size might work to her advantage as well. She was not by any stretch dainty, but she was a handsome woman of sorts and practical of nature.

'I can't say, Georgina, but why indeed. That is the question,' Mrs Lawson said. 'I am sure some of you remember the case – I believe the lady, according to today's *Brisbane Courier*, is Mrs Hilda Rodgers, of West End.'

There were more gasps and nods of agreement. Matilda knew the name and not just from reading it this morning, but could not recall any incident related to the deceased.

Alice looked at her with a blank expression, which was not surprising given Alice had come to Australia from England but six months ago.

Mrs Lawson continued. 'Betty, you remember the case, don't you? Perhaps you can share what you know, and then we can determine what angles we should take to report on this story from a woman's perspective. Our readers will expect some comment from us.'

'Of course, Mrs Lawson,' Betty said, and looked at the faces in front of her. Mrs Lawson always encouraged others to shine, and Betty was pleased with the opportunity to address the group.

'About six months ago, Mrs Rodgers – Hilda – went to

trial to try to change the law after her husband placed her in an asylum and there was absolutely nothing wrong with her, a conclusion which members of the jury quickly arrived at as well.'

There was much tittering and shaking of heads by the women at the table. Betty continued. 'Her husband, Mr Rodgers, is twenty years her senior and a strict disciplinarian, according to the information that came out at her trial. So strict that one of their children was hospitalised after a beating. Of course, Hilda abhorred this behaviour and while she feared Mr Rodgers, one day she took it upon herself to challenge him. She was no stranger to her husband's disciplinary ways either and felt the wrath of his anger many a time.'

'How many children did they have?' the receptionist asked.

'Four, I believe,' Betty said and looked to Mrs Lawson for confirmation.

'Yes, four. Three boys and a girl. The daughter passed away from influenza before she reached double figures and the youngest, a boy, seemed to be particularly vulnerable to his father's discipline – I understand he was a slow learner,' Mrs Lawson said.

'Hilda sought help from a doctor,' Betty said, 'but the doctor turned on her and advised her husband. He then furnished the husband with the relevant medical paperwork that asserted Hilda was overtaxed and unable to function, and the police removed her to an insane asylum.'

Matilda's hand went straight to her heart – the thought so terrifying. 'Could no one speak for her?' she asked.

Betty shook her head. 'No one was successful initially. She had a cousin and friends who attempted to assist, but Mr Rodgers was a respected and powerful figure in the community. He is retired now, but at the time he was a principal at one of the private boys' colleges.'

'Goodness, one can only imagine what the students endured, too,' Alice said.

'Indeed,' Mrs Lawson said, and appeared keen to move the discussion along. 'There are probably many women now in mental asylums who have undergone the same fate and it would require the commitment of a passionate group of women, and men, to see justice for them, but in Hilda's case, she spent three years in the asylum. She was only recently released when her eldest son turned twenty-one and could sign her out.'

'But where did she go on release? She would not have had her own means and could not return home, surely,' Georgina asked.

Betty agreed. 'From what I recall from the trial, Hilda stayed with a cousin. That cousin had been petitioning a judge to have her released and so the matter went before a court. She was released to her own care. That was about six months ago now.'

There was a silence around the table as each of the ladies contemplated the fate of Mrs Hilda Rodgers, now free, but for some reason, had chosen to throw herself to her death.

'We don't know what might have driven Hilda to take the violent step and depart this earth, but I imagine the police will investigate,' Mrs Lawson said with a glance to Matilda.

'Or perhaps they won't. Perhaps it will be grounds for her husband to prove he was right all along, and she should have remained in care. Let us discuss how we will represent this story.' Mrs Lawson turned to the senior writers seated on her right.

Matilda did not reveal that Thomas was on his way to the coroner this morning to view Mrs Hilda Rodgers. This will be telling, she thought – will Thomas consider the case worthy of the police's attention, or will Hilda be filed as a woman who had lost her way?

Chapter 5

Aunt Audrey – Mrs Samuel Bloomfield – was applying her gloves when Matilda arrived home that evening. Matilda recognised the impressive carriage waiting in the driveway of the Hayward family's Highgate Hill home. She took a deep breath for fortitude, pushed open the front door and braced herself for the expected inquisition.

'Ah Matilda, good, I had hoped to catch you before I left,' Aunt Audrey said, allowing Matilda to plant a kiss upon her cheek. Harriet stood nearby, holding Aunt Audrey's hat.

'Hello, Aunt and Harriet, what a lovely winter evening,' Matilda said, removing her own hat and patting down her hair.

'Yes, and high time you were home, young lady,' Aunt Audrey took the opportunity to remind her. 'It gets dark so early and you should not be out unaccompanied. There are so many unsavoury characters around these days. Speaking of which, has Thomas discussed your betrothal yet?'

'I'm not sure Thomas would like to be thought of as

unsavoury,' Matilda teased her aunt as Harriet restrained herself from smiling.

Aunt Audrey gave her a small smile. 'I am expecting him to save you from unsavoury types, make a decent woman of you.'

'Oh, dear, what a challenge.' Matilda did her best not to sigh. 'But no, we have not discussed our future since I saw you on Sunday, Aunt. We are not in any hurry.'

'Well, I most certainly am, and I suspect your father feels the same,' she said, with a glance at her brother's office behind the stairwell. 'We are not getting any younger and it is my duty, in remembrance of your dear mother, to see you suitably matched.'

Matilda softened. 'Thank you, Aunt. I will do my best to relieve you of that responsibility before we are both too old to celebrate a wedding. Are you not staying for dinner?'

'No dear, I have church choir rehearsal tonight. Thank you, Harriet,' she said, taking her hat from Harriet's hands. 'I have just been here having a word with Mary about this year's entry into the annual exhibition in August.'

'But it is weeks away.'

'And there is no time to waste. One does not win by being unprepared.'

'Of course,' Matilda agreed and walked her aunt outside to the waiting carriage. After waving her off, she returned inside, and Mary put her head around the kitchen door.

'All clear, Mary,' Matilda assured the cook, and Mary chuckled.

'What is it to be this year?' Matilda asked.

'The same as always, lass – my Irish shortbread biscuits. Why change a good thing when yer on a winner, as my father used to say? Mind you, he was at the races when he said that and never had much luck.'

Matilda and Harriet laughed.

'Did Aunt Audrey try to steal you away again?' Matilda asked, narrowing her eyes.

'Aye, she did. She's persistent, I'll give her that. Dinner in fifteen minutes, corn beef and white sauce with all the trimmings,' Cook said and disappeared again back into the kitchen from where the delicious smells of dinner emanated.

Matilda and Harriet turned as the front door barged open and Elijah and his twin, Gideon, entered.

'Both home for dinner!' Harriet exclaimed as Mr Hayward emerged from his office to join his family. 'The shock,' she said in jest and put her hand to her heart.

The men laughed.

'We like to keep you and Cook on your toes,' Gideon teased Harriet. 'Smells good.'

'I shall go and tell Cook not to expect to serve corn beef sandwiches for the rest of the week. She will be pleased. Dinner in fifteen minutes, Mr Hayward, if that is suitable?' Harriet said and on receiving his thanks, departed.

'How was your first day at the asylum, Elijah?' Matilda asked

'The place is a mad house,' he joked.

'Come, we'll seat ourselves in the dining room, have a small drink and hear about it, shall we?' Mr Hayward suggested.

The front door opened again, and Matilda smiled with delight.

'Daniel too, what a treat. Pa, you won't have to put up with just my company tonight,' she teased.

'Fine company it is, any night,' Mr Hayward said and offered Matilda his arm as they moved to the dining room.

Once seated and refreshed, the family pumped Elijah with questions.

'Yes, he's likeable, my new supervisor – Dr Stephen O'Shea. He's about seven feet, or maybe he just seems that way because he's lanky too, but a pleasant fellow. He has a few interesting views on matters, too delicate to mention here,' Elijah said with a glance at Matilda, who rolled her eyes. 'I haven't met my counterpart, the other doctor who looks after the men's ward, yet.'

Harriet entered with Mary's dishes of steaming vegetables and meat, and passed them to the boys.

'Did you meet any really odd ones?' his twin, Gideon, asked.

'Yes, there's definitely insane people living there,' Elijah said and gave his twin a grin. 'Hence the name, the Asylum for the Insane.'

Matilda cut to the chase. 'What of the lady who fell to her death, Elijah – Mrs Hilda Rodgers – was there any talk of her? She spent some time in your asylum.'

'Ah, I thought I knew the name,' Mr Hayward said. 'I couldn't recall in what legal circles I had heard it. Mrs Rodgers was the lady who took her husband to court to prove her sanity after he locked her away.'

'That is her, Pa,' Matilda said. 'There was much talk about it today at the *Women's Journal*. Mrs Lawson and our deputy editor, Betty, well remembered the case.'

'Her son got her out, did he not?' Daniel asked.

'Yes. She has not been out for long, I believe, and now this…' Matilda said.

Elijah accepted a serving of potatoes and then responded to Matilda. 'There was little said in the morning, but by the afternoon when the staff and even some patients made the connection, there was definitely fascination about her death.'

'What did the staff have to say?' Matilda asked.

'You can't report this, Tillie,' Elijah said, using her nickname with affection.

'Of course not,' she agreed. 'Consider it research.' Finishing a bite, Matilda placed her knife and fork down and gave Elijah her full attention.

'Well, several of the nurses were quite shocked. They agreed she had always been sane and just locked up at the cruel whim of her husband.'

'I don't know how anyone could do that to a person you married and professed to love,' Daniel interrupted.

'And even if you fell out of love, you promised to have and to hold, for better or for worse,' Gideon said, agreeing with his elder brother. All eyes turned to him.

'What?' he asked.

'I thought for sure you would have said something in jest, Gids, such as the asylum being man's best friend or similar,' Matilda said, surprised.

He gave a small shrug. 'After spending a few hours in a lockup – Elijah's fault leading me astray with drink,' he said with a glance and grin to his twin, 'I cannot imagine how a sane person could survive any sort of incarceration.'

'Terrible indeed,' Mr Hayward agreed. 'Sadly, many marriages are more for convenience and comfort than for love. Not that there is a right or wrong reason for marriage, but love or at least respect, mutual admiration and affection is always desirable and ensures a happier long-term marriage.'

'Did you always love Mother, Pa, or did it start as affection?' Matilda asked, even though she knew the answer in her heart, she was keen to hear her father speak of the mother she barely knew and lost at the age of four. Amos, the eldest, then 12, and Daniel at eight, remembered her best. All eyes turned to Mr Hayward.

'From the moment I laid eyes upon your mother, Matilda, she was my sun and my moon,' he said, and Matilda smiled with delight.

'What about the lunatics? What did they have to say about the woman's death?' Gideon asked, the question truer to his character.

'Of the 200 in my care, I met about fifty today,' Elijah said. 'There are some gentle souls there, but only a couple were lucid enough to understand – they overhead the nurses, I believe. I gained no insights from them other than it saddened them a friend had passed away. But there is good news for Matilda.'

'I can come in with you?' she asked excitedly.

'More or less. There is a volunteer program. It might be an excellent chance for you to meet some patients without trailing behind me.'

Matilda clapped her hands. 'Wonderful. I shall discuss it with Mrs Lawson and volunteer perhaps on the days I am not working. What say you, Pa?'

'If you like and Elijah is confident of your safety, I don't see why not,' Mr Hayward answered.

'Don't drag Alice there,' Daniel grumbled, referring to his love interest, whom he had met through Matilda. 'I don't want to be regaled with tales of the mad.'

'Why not?' Matilda asked. 'She's a fine writer and would relish the chance, I'm sure. But you need not worry, she is quite tied up reporting for the Women's Suffrage Society at the moment. I will find another victim,' she teased.

'Speaking of the ladies,' Gideon cut in, 'this morning I met a lady seeking your whereabouts, brother.'

Elijah and Daniel both looked at him with blank expressions, and Gideon continued. 'You are safe Dan; she was seeking Elijah. A Miss Lily Chappell came into my gallery.'

Elijah groaned, and the family chuckled.

'I thought I had lost her since moving from the doctor's general practice to the asylum.'

'Apparently not,' Gideon said. 'She was there to view the artwork with her mother and on seeing my name on the door was most excited that we were related, and twins at that. She even assured me that while we are not identical, I am just as handsome.' Gideon grinned.

'I am not in the least interested in Miss Chappell,' Elijah assured his twin.

'I am pleased to hear that,' Gideon said.

'Oh no, tell me you did not let Miss Chappell know where I am working? She might try to get admitted,' Elijah said in jest.

'On the contrary. She is exceedingly pretty, lively and I believe wealthy,' Gideon said. 'I asked her to lunch on Saturday!'

Chapter 6

A bell tinkled lightly as Detective Ashdown and Detective Dart entered the small bakery. Harry Dart held the door open for a senior lady as she departed with a box of fresh baked goods and her thanks to the handsome mature man holding the door for her.

'Good morning, gentleman,' a young, fair-haired man said, wiping his hands down the front of his industrial apron. Behind him, Thomas could see two more young men at work – one kneading dough, and the other checking trays in the oven. While they were not all similar of colouring, it was clear from their features they were brothers.

'Good morning,' Thomas said as he moved to the counter, avoiding brushing against it in his dark suit for fear of attracting flour dust. He introduced himself and Detective Dart. 'We are seeking a word with Mr Silas Rodgers, son of Mrs Hilda Rodgers.'

The young man straightened. 'That would be me, Detective,' he said.

'Good morning to you,' Harry said. 'Are these your brothers slaving away back there?' he asked with a smile.

Silas relaxed a little. 'Yes, the taller one is Claude, and that's Jesse at the oven.'

'We are sorry to learn of the death of your mother, Mr Rodgers,' Thomas said, remembering to show some empathy before targeting the young man with questions. Harry, his mentor, was slowly rubbing off on him.

Silas nodded and swallowed. 'Thank you. You can call me Silas. So, you're here about that?'

'Yes. A few questions, if we may?' Thomas asked.

Silas looked confused. 'But Mum took her own life. It is a crime but there is no one to punish except our father who, believe me, feels no guilt in this matter and accepts no responsibility.'

The bell tinkled as two ladies entered together, laughing. Silas turned to his brothers. Claude had his hands in the dough.

'Jesse, shop,' he said, and his brother appeared to assist the ladies. Silas tipped his head, indicating a back room and the two men followed him to a side exit. They entered a small office with several chairs and a desk and considerable paperwork that no doubt was not a priority to the young men. All three were seated before Silas added, 'There were witnesses who saw her jump.'

Thomas nodded. 'It is peculiar that after all the years of struggle to be free of the asylum, enduring the public humiliation of a court case and earning her freedom, that your mother would then take her own life, do you not think?'

'I couldn't agree with you more. My brothers and I are at a loss to understand it.' He looked away momentarily towards a small window while settling his emotions. The door burst open, and his brother Claude stuck his head in.

'All okay, Sil?' he asked with a glance at the detectives. Silas nodded.

'It's about Mum. I'll explain later.'

His brother eyed the two detectives again and retreated, closing the door behind him.

'You've done well for yourself here, lad,' Harry said, and Silas smiled.

'I finished my bakery apprenticeship last year and I'm renting the premises. We're keeping our heads above water,' he said. 'I hope to own it one day.'

'And you've apprenticed both of your brothers?' Thomas asked.

Silas nodded. 'It gets them away from our father. We now have incomes and are not dependent on him. We live upstairs and work downstairs.'

'You're an impressive young man.' Harry praised him and Silas coloured with the praise, seldom received.

'Where was your mother living when you secured her release?' Thomas asked.

'With my aunt, her cousin, Flora. She's the one who helped me and petitioned the judge.'

'I'd like to have a word to her too, if you could give me her address?' Thomas said and Silas obliged.

'I don't understand, Detectives, what are you looking for. Has something happened?'

Thomas explained. 'It may be that your mother took her own life, Silas, but with two more deaths in the last fortnight, both from falls at the same place—'

'Were the other deaths unexpected too?' he interrupted.

'Not necessarily. One was a troubled soul from what we understand,' Harry answered.

'We just want to be sure before we close the case,' Thomas said.

'Thank you,' Silas said, understanding and grateful for their attention to his mother.

Thomas continued. 'Your mother had fresh bruises and a mark on her wrist, which might indicate a struggle. It may not have occurred as a result of her bridge fall, however.'

Silas nodded and leaned forward on the desk, webbing his fingers in front of him.

'Mum returned home to get some clothing and personal items. Flora went with her, but my father asked Flora to wait outside so he could have a private word with my mother. Flora said he looked contrite. That was short-lived. He hit Mum again and continued until Flora got one of the house staff to let her in.'

'Was he capable of contrition? Did he want your mother to return to the marriage?' Harry asked.

'The only thing my father is capable of is wielding his power. It is a testimony to her she lasted with him as long as she did,' Silas said. 'It was not love, just duty. He threatened that if Mum left him, she would never see us boys again.'

'How do your brothers feel about the situation?' Thomas asked.

'Claude – he's 19 – and was very close to Mum… he's really sad but he won't show it. He's just working all the time. Jesse's eighteen and the youngest. He's boiling over. I'm watching him like a hawk; I just hope he doesn't do anything we'll all regret.'

*****

'They are fine boys,' Harry said as the two men walked up the path to the Bowen Hills residence of the boys' father and Hilda's husband – Mr Raymond Rodgers.

'A credit to their mother, for sure,' Thomas said in agreement. 'Can you believe you could have three boys and a wife and be so unloved by them?' His voice faded off. It was a safe home Thomas grew up in, but never a loving one. It would not be the home he intended to create for his future family, he would ensure that.

Harry knocked, and the men waited as a house steward advised Mr Rodgers of their arrival, without an appointment, as he pointed out.

A tall, solid man came to the door. Well-groomed, early sixties and whiskered, he did not invite the men inside and insisted on seeing their identification.

'What is this about then?'

'Our condolences on the passing of Mrs Rodgers,' Harry said.

Mr Rodgers nodded and said no more.

'We're enquiring as to the state of mind of your wife immediately before her death and the fresh bruising on her body,' Thomas said.

'State of her mind?' Mr Rodgers said and gave a humourless laugh. 'She should never have been allowed out of the asylum. She was never a well woman… nerves, insecurity, manic behaviour.'

'And the bruises?' Harry cut to the chase.

'I did my best to maintain a stable and orderly household.'

'Your sons have moved out?' Thomas asked, knowing the answer.

'Everything I did for those boys and their mother was aimed to develop character and prepare the boys to contribute to society. The bible says, "Foolishness is bound in the heart of a child; but the rod of correction shall drive it far from him." They got nothing that they did not need or deserve.'

Thomas glanced at Harry. There was nothing to be gained here and after a few more questions that yielded little information, they bade Mr Rodgers good day.

When they were far enough away, Thomas said: 'The Bible is very convenient… there is always something that can be adapted.'

'Indeed. I remember an appropriate verse that begins "Whoever receives one such child in my name receives me". I'm not sure the good Lord would approve of the reception he would get if he were a child in the residence of Mr Rodgers.'

Thomas felt a desperate need to see and touch Matilda. He silently gave thanks that Mr Hayward was such a gentle soul and had never raised a hand to his daughter or sons.

'I want to know more about the first woman who fell to

her death,' Thomas said, thinking out loud to push Matilda from his mind. 'We need to talk with the cousin, Flora, and we should visit the hospital where Mrs Hilda Rodgers died.'

'Yes,' Harry agreed. 'Perhaps the staff can tell us if Hilda had any last words.'

'Such as "my husband pushed me". Now that would be helpful,' Thomas said, and Harry chuckled beside him.

'Love your optimism, Thom. If only.' He glanced back at the house in the distance. 'I wonder if the boys will ever take retribution into their own hands.'

Thomas shook his head. 'I have read that abuse victims are often so systemically fearful of their abuser, that it prevents them from acting when they see the person they most fear.'

Harry looked impressed.

'*The Bulletin* had an interesting article on it.'

'And you found time to read it?' Harry asked, eyebrows raised in surprise. 'You're an ambitious young man, Thom. You remind me of myself in my early years, only you have more skill now than I ever had. I wouldn't want to be a criminal in Brisbane on your shift.'

Thomas laughed and looked embarrassed. Like the Rodgers brothers, he rarely received encouragement or praise from his own father, and he had little idea how to respond to it.

Chapter 7

Matilda felt nervous as she waited for her turn. All the young ladies did… except for a couple of very confident ladies who loved their minute in the spotlight.

The weekly meeting for the *Women's Journal* part-time and junior staff was now in session and Mrs Lawson invited each lady around the table to discuss her current workload, pitch a story, or update her on the progress if she were already working on a project. It was also a good chance for Mrs Lawson to monitor her younger, less experienced charges, such as Matilda and Alice, and several of the apprentices in the printing area.

Sandwiched between her writing friend, Alice, and Georgina, an illustrator, Matilda noted Georgina did not appear in the slightest bit nervous. Matilda focused to settle her nerves; Alice was speaking of her ongoing women's suffrage reporting.

'Betty has given me several of the papers we have received from the Washington Conference of Women, Mrs Lawson.

As you know, but the ladies might not—' she looked at the faces around the table '—the conference is discussing ways to advance women's interests, including female suffrage.'

'Anything of particular interest thus far, Alice?' Mrs Lawson asked. She liked to challenge the ladies to find an angle and be succinct, plus it was an excellent opportunity to see where each staff members' passion lay.

'Indeed, Mrs Lawson. I don't have all the papers yet but the education paper and that on professions are fascinating,' Alice said in her crisp British accent. 'It appears that in many workplaces, there is a firm belief that women have no rights whatsoever and attempts to legislate these rights is seen by some employers as a gross interference with constitutional rights!'

'Goodness, have you ever heard of such a thing?' Mrs Lawson said under her breath.

Alice shook her head. 'Betty has asked me to condense the speakers' papers into articles for our readers,' she finished.

'Excellent,' Mrs Lawson said.

The women around the table all agreed that was most interesting. Matilda drew a deep breath to calm herself, knowing she was next to speak.

'Matilda, how is your week looking and what have you for us today?' Mrs Lawson asked.

'I hoped, Mrs Lawson, considering the recent death of Mrs Hilda Rodgers, that you might think this suggestion is valid.' Matilda briefly mentioned the volunteer program at the asylum and how volunteering out of work hours might benefit her writing and provide content for the journal, such as an article on life in an asylum or select profile pieces on female inmates or staff. She also mentioned Elijah's role to ensure all the cards were on the table.

'It sounds rather intriguing,' Mrs Lawson said, 'and an excellent opportunity to understand the condition and characters within those walls.'

The ladies around the table agreed as Mrs Lawson thought for a moment and then added, 'I will contact the asylum as we need to be transparent. We will aim for sympathetic articles, and I will speak with whoever is in charge to gain permission for you to do your interviews and observations.'

'Transparency would be a relief,' Matilda agreed.

Mrs Lawson nodded. 'Let's set aside a month. Come in for our daily meetings, and then spend the afternoon of your shift volunteering at the asylum. After a few weeks and with a few articles underway, if you wish to continue to volunteer, you could do that in your own time.'

'That would be wonderful, thank you, Mrs Lawson.'

'I don't like you to go unaccompanied, although the volunteer program is most likely well managed,' Mrs Lawson said.

Alice, beside Matilda, looked crestfallen that they could not work this story together. They had been a formidable team on their last few stories when visiting the freak show and reporting on the passionate scandal of the artist's muse.

'Perhaps one of the ladies might accompany you and provide a different insight?' Mrs Lawson looked around the table.

'Ooh, I'd love to do that,' Georgina Urry said with

enthusiasm, offering herself.

'That's a splendid idea, Georgina,' Mrs Lawson said, pleased. 'Then we will have illustrations to accompany the articles. I shall check with Ruth that she can spare you.' She made another note in her book.

'It will be a good experience for me too, and let me showcase some more pieces in my folio,' Georgina added. 'I could volunteer to do some art classes with the ladies, while drawing them myself.'

'There you go,' Mrs Lawson smiled, satisfied, placing her pencil down. 'Then both of you will spend two afternoons a week for one month at the asylum, if we are permitted to do so, and create some wonderful content for the journal.'

Matilda and Georgina smiled happily at each other. Matilda was relieved that Georgina put her hand up – she liked the frank, witty and funny woman. She had given little thought, however, to what she might encounter in the asylum, but Mrs Lawson had.

'If you solve the mystery of Mrs Rodgers' death while there, do give it to us before your detective,' she said with a smile to Matilda, which brought a round of nudges and laughter from the ladies.

Chapter 8

Dr Elijah Hayward's counterpart from the male ward of the Asylum for the Insane – Dr Victor McQuade – was of equal age to Elijah, but a man short of appearance and patience. Elijah suspected their boss, Dr Stephen O'Shea, hadn't noticed, being so gregarious himself. Perhaps the reason he had hired two staff members who at best could be described as introverted and, at worst in the case of Victor, sullen, was to ensure he remained the most popular. A petty thought, Elijah knew, but to see Dr O'Shea in action, one would think he had to be the centre of attention at all times when surely the patients should be. Elijah was no stranger to that with a twin and another brother equally loud as his new boss. Not that he minded; he was comfortable taking the back seat and not in need of the spotlight.

'Well, it is great to have a full team again,' Dr O'Shea was saying looking from Elijah to Victor and back. As they walked through the male wards, Dr O'Shea invited Victor to provide his daily update on patients. Elijah joined them, observing the patients and conditions should he need to tend to anyone on the night shift or fill in as required.

'Two deaths this week, both expected,' Victor reported. 'Age and exhaustion.'

Dr O'Shea nodded. 'Any trouble?'

'No more than usual. Five new admissions so I am progressing them now and will determine the best residential and work paths for them by the end of the week.'

'Excellent.' Dr O'Shea nodded.

'Good morning, gentleman,' an elderly patient said, passing them with a doff of his hat.

'Good morning, Rupert. How is your business today?' Dr O'Shea asked the well-dressed older man.

'Progressing well, sir, I thank you,' he said and continued on his path.

'Beyond redemption,' Dr O'Shea said for Elijah's ears. 'He lost his family's fortune in a poor business decision and then penniless, his wife deserted him, and he had a breakdown, poor fellow. Now, every day, he believes he is still maintaining his line of industry.' Dr O'Shea sighed and shook his head. 'The injustice of life.' Then he brightened. 'But onward, shall we?'

They finished their rounds and Victor declined the invitation to escort the two men on the rounds of the women's ward.

'As I am familiar with the women's wards, I shall leave you to it and tend my new admissions, if that is acceptable?' Victor said.

'Of course,' Dr O'Shea said, and arranged a time later with Victor to discuss his fresh cases.

'Good day to you, Elijah and welcome,' Victor said curtly and departed.

When he was out of earshot, Dr O'Shea said, 'He is a very capable young doctor, but as you can see, his bedside manner needs a little work. Still, this is a good place for a doctor who does not need to pay courtesy to everyday customers.'

'I imagine so,' Elijah agreed. 'After all, the patients have no choice but to come back, and their referrals will not assist us much.'

Dr O'Shea laughed. 'Exactly. Now tell me who you have found to be your most interesting patient?' he asked as they walked towards Elijah's wing.

'So many to choose from,' Elijah said and made the doctor laugh again. 'You are right about what you said on my first day though.'

'Do tell?'

'Some ladies seem very sane. Tell me if you will as a point of interest, I understand Mrs Hilda Rodgers was a patient here. Did you think she belonged here?' Elijah asked, not necessarily intending to tell Matilda or Thomas, but purely from professional curiosity.

'I thought she should never have been released,' Dr O'Shea said most seriously. 'And it looks as if I was right.'

They passed through the section of the women's asylum for violent patients, finding everything in order, and made their way to the long-term and chronic residents' section. The two doctors entered a room where the resident nurse had gathered half a dozen patients requiring attention.

'Good morning Nurse Hopkins,' Dr O'Shea said with a booming voice and a large grin. 'You look as lovely this morning as the day itself.'

Nurse Hopkins, a kind, motherly, middle-aged nurse, laughed with pleasure.

'Go on with you, Doctor. You know how to make my day. Good morning to you too, Dr Hayward,' she said, giving Elijah a warm smile.

'Good morning, Nurse Hopkins, and thank you for being so organised,' he said noting the patients needing attention were waiting, their dressings, medications and charts on hand.

'The ladies helped, didn't you, my dears?' she said, turning to the patients who sat watching attentively.

One lady clapped her hands and repeated, 'We helped, we helped.'

Elijah gave her a smile and nodded.

Dr O'Shea greeted the ladies and remembered a few facts about each to make small talk with them before departing with a wave and leaving Elijah to finish his work. With so many patients, Elijah considered it an impressive act on Dr O'Shea's part, but then again, the ladies were long-term residents.

Elijah gently lowered himself in the chair in front of his first patient – he had learned as early as his first day, it was better not to do anything quickly or with sharp movements as it caused alarm. He studied Hannah, an Irish woman in her fifties from County Cork, and requesting her arm, he removed the dressing binding half of it. Beside him, in his peripheral vision, he could see one lady swaying back and forward in constant motion, another hummed a hymn he recognised from church, and the patient in the far corner sat as still as a statue, as if by not moving, no one would know she was there.

Elijah noted that Nurse Hopkins, like most women, was most capable of multi-tasking – keeping a watchful eye on the ladies and attuned to his needs.

'Is it causing you pain, Hannah?' he asked as he cleaned and redress the wound.

'I've lots of aches and pains, Doctor, so no more than any of the others are,' she said, watching him.

'I hear you are very good at gardening. How did it happen again?' he asked. Elijah knew, but he liked to engage the women in conversation to test their lucidity and get to know their limitations a little better.

'I am just that, good at gardening, I am,' she agreed. 'But I was talking with the herbs I was and tending them when I fell… 'twas the garden bed's fault for tripping me.'

Elijah nodded. 'Ah yes, they do that, they can be quite cunning.'

Nurse Hopkins suppressed a laugh as Hannah nodded earnestly.

'You've met it then?' she asked.

'Not that one, but I know a few garden beds,' Elijah assured her.

'Do you have a sweetheart, Doctor?' she asked, and Elijah noticed the amused look and raised eyebrow from Nurse Hopkins, keen to see how he handled this one.

'I do indeed,' he said, embellishing the truth for fear Hannah would offer to take the role. 'A lovely lady she is, too good for me,' he said with a smile to Hannah.

'I had a sweetheart,' Hannah said and sighed. 'But he died.'

'I am sorry to hear that, Hannah. I hope your memories of him are dear to you.' He sat back after securing the bandage. 'There you go, it's healing nicely. We'll see you again tomorrow then.'

'I should be available tomorrow, but I'll have to check,' Hannah said. 'Thank you, Doctor.'

She rose and Nurse Hopkins whispered conspiratorially to Elijah, 'Don't be too sorry, she poisoned him.'

Elijah's shocked expression engaged another laugh from Nurse Hopkins as she went to the doorway to organise an orderly to escort Hannah back to the garden.

'Good grief,' Elijah muttered under his breath as he moved to his next patient, Meredith. She was a tall, graceful and softly spoken woman with high cheekbones that once would have made her a beautiful young woman. Elijah learned she had been a professional dressmaker but suffered terrible burns and trauma in a fire. To look at her, one would never know, as the wounds were below the neck and covered by her high-neck frock and apron.

Let's hope she's not capable of murder, he thought.

'Good morning, Meredith, how are you feeling today?' Elijah asked, studying the woman and briefly consulting her file.

'I had some trouble breathing last night,' she said, slowly

moving her hand to her chest, and Elijah leaned forward to catch her words.

'Are you breathing easier now?' he asked.

'Yes. It comes and goes.' She stretched her fingers.

'Are you experiencing pain in your hands or joints?' Elijah asked, expecting always to have to simplify his questions, but Meredith's response showed she understood him clearly.

'More so of late,' she said. 'As if they are frozen or have pins and needles.'

Elijah nodded and Nurse Hopkins offered, 'Meredith works every day in the sewing room, making the clothing all the residents are wearing, and she makes some beautiful dolls from material scraps, don't you, Meredith?'

Meredith nodded and blushed with the praise.

'I am not sure that I will be able to fly though, as expected,' she said.

Her response took Elijah by surprise when the conversation had been progressing well until then.

'I think it is best to leave the flying to the birds, don't you?' he suggested gently. 'They have the wings for it.'

'But I am growing wings too, that's why I have back pain, I am sure. They are not developed yet. Dr O'Shea says if we believe in anything hard enough, we can make it happen.'

Elijah glanced at Nurse Hopkins and back at Meredith. He had to be careful not to contradict his boss.

'And that is very good advice indeed. But let's make sure those wings are fully formed first and then we can talk about flying.' He asked some more questions about her condition, undertook some rudimentary tests, including listening to her heart and taking Meredith's temperature, and released her with a request to see her again tomorrow or sooner if she should have breathing problems again. He noted this on her file and for the night nurse to check on her.

After Meredith's departure, Elijah spoke to the nurse in a quiet voice. 'There are no outlets where Meredith could attempt to fly and throw herself from, are there?'

'Not anymore,' Nurse Hopkin's said. 'They have all been boarded up or sealed. We've also fenced the waterhole. Several patients thought they were mermaids.'

They shared a smile with no malice intended.

'Just your average day at the asylum,' she said to him with a wink.

Chapter 9

Thomas had a particularly sensitive nose… the smell of a death scene was bad enough, but the smell of blood – a thin, cloying, metallic smell, never left him – it was one that his partner, Harry, could never detect. But on entering the hospital, even Harry blanched at the heavy smell of disinfectant.

'Probably for the best,' Harry said. 'No point going to hospital and getting sick.'

'Perish the thought,' Thomas said. He stood beside his partner at the front desk and watched the coming-and-goings as Harry made their enquiries.

'You're in luck!' the receptionist said as if they had won the local raffle. 'The nurse who was with Mrs Rodgers is on today… if you'd come yesterday, I would have had to send you home empty-handed.'

'Our lucky day,' Harry agreed with a grin, admiring the cheery receptionist – just what every hospital needed to brighten the load. She was no beauty, but her manner and smile transformed her.

'Take a seat, gents. I'll get Nurse Morgan,' the receptionist said and hailed a passing nurse to carry the message.

Thomas sat as far away as he could from the patients waiting in the sitting room, and Harry grinned as he joined him.

'I didn't know you had such an aversion to hospitals. Do you want to wait outside?' Harry asked.

'Tempting, but I'll see it through,' Thomas said. 'I just think it's stupid to come to a place where everyone is sick unless you're sick or working here.'

A nurse hurried towards them, giving the impression she was far too busy to be interrupted.

The two men rose.

'I'm Nurse Morgan. May I be of assistance?'

'Please,' Thomas said and introduced himself and Harry. 'Can we talk in private?'

'The exit is closer, so let's step into the garden,' she suggested, to Thomas's delight.

Harry explained their reason for being on site.

'Of course I remember Mrs Rodgers, that poor woman,' she said, folding her arms across her chest in an act of protecting herself. Thomas estimated she was in her early thirties despite grey hairs appearing around her temple. She wore no wedding band.

'Was anyone with her when she arrived or before she died, other than the medical teams?' Thomas asked.

'Other than myself, no. I believe there were people by her side after she was brought to the river's edge, but none of them came to the hospital with her.'

'Did she say anything at all, any last words or impressions that you got from her?' Harry asked, sounding desperate.

'Yes,' Nurse Morgan said, 'she did. She said one thing only before passing away.'

The two men watched her in heightened anticipation.

'She said "*fly*".'

*****

Flora Bignell's town home was charming, to say the least. Across the river in the unfashionable streets, she had made it look its best with a garden in bloom inside and outside. She served the two detectives tea while Thomas studied the thin, neat woman who was short on frills but appeared to have done the best she could with her limited purse.

'Poor Hilda had a terrible life,' her cousin explained. 'Her parents insisted she marry Raymond – mature, successful, clever, and as we soon found out, he brought his work home with him. If he wasn't beating those poor students at his school, he was beating his wife and sons.'

She sat down after pouring three cups of tea and pushed the biscuits towards the men. Harry happily accepted; it was a long time since breakfast.

'Do you know what she was doing that day on the Victoria Bridge, and if she was alone?' Thomas asked, stirring milk into his tea.

'I can't honestly say. She told me she was going for a walk and that was the last time I saw her. I don't know why she went there or if she was meeting anyone there. Hilda wasn't a prisoner in my home. She was a free woman. Daily she would drop into the bakery to see the boys.'

'Did she not want to work there with them? I imagine they could have used the help and free labour?' Harry asked.

'Oh, she desperately wanted to work there,' Flora said, sitting back in her chair and pushing a strand of her hair behind her ears. 'But when she first started working in the shop it caused too many problems.'

'How so?' Thomas asked.

'Many people wanted to see her and speak with her as she had become quite recognisable after the trial. Women sharing their own nightmare stories, people congratulating her, others, especially men, saying they wouldn't frequent a store where a woman did not know her place and so on. It wasn't good for custom, and it was driving away the business that the boys had established.'

Harry nodded. 'So, she thought it best for the boys if she stayed away.'

'Yes. But she went in twice a week to do the books, as she could do that from the back room, and no one knew she was there.' Flora sighed. 'How she loved those boys.'

'Why? Why did she do it?' Thomas asked, frustrated.

'I wish I could tell you why,' Flora said and ran her hand over her forehead. 'She was safe and wanted here. I am a widow, and I was pleased with her company. Her boys were safe.' She shook her head. 'I have gone over and over her death in my head a thousand times. Why now?'

'Exactly our predicament,' Harry agreed. 'Did you see any signs of decline in her at all?'

'Not mentally, but definitely physically. She was tired, and she said she was having some chest pains, some trouble breathing,' Flora explained. 'She was intending to go to the doctor. But now…' Flora sighed, 'she will feel no more pain evermore.'

Chapter 10

Thomas was silent as the men caught an omnibus back to the office.

'Don't dwell on it too much, Thom,' Harry said. 'Life is full of injustices, and we can't fix them all. Let's just hope to bring about an appropriate punishment where we can and some peace to the family.'

'Sometimes, I just want to hit someone,' Thomas said and made Harry chuckle. 'I can think of several people right now I'd line up for a thrashing and Raymond Rodgers is in the front of the queue.'

'You know what you need, lad, to see the lovely Miss Hayward,' Harry said. 'Get a reminder in your life that there's plenty of goodness and sweetness out there in the world.'

'Maybe you are right,' Thomas said, not one to talk about matters of the heart.

'Let's call it a day and start fresh tomorrow. Swing by now and see if you can enjoy a dusk stroll together,

I always find that to possess great therapeutic efficacy,' Harry said, speaking from experience with a marriage that had endured decades.

Thomas had to admit that sounded appealing. At the station, he bade good evening to his partner and proceeded to the Hayward household. He stopped on the way to purchase a large bouquet of red roses to present to Matilda and suffered the smiles of every woman he passed on the way to see her.

'She's not home yet, Thom,' Harriet said with a shake of her head and frustration in her voice. 'Come in and wait. I'll make you some tea, or Mr Hayward will be back from his walk shortly and he'll be happy to have a drinking friend.'

'Ah, thank you, Harriet, but I'll head home and check on that nephew of mine,' Thomas said, handing over the roses for Matilda.

'You spoil her,' Harriet said.

'She is worth it,' Thomas said with a smile.

'That she is.'

Bidding Harriet farewell, he returned his hat to his head and headed up the path and out the gates of the Hayward property, disappointment overriding him, but he did not want to sit in wait, when she may return tired from her day. One day, she would be at home waiting for him, and he hoped it would be sooner than later. He made his way to the omnibus.

*****

Matilda had only just thought of Thomas when she set eyes on him, leaving through the gate of her home. He had not seen her as yet and for a moment she studied him as a stranger might. He was tall, well-groomed, his shoulders wide, and his face so handsome.

'Thomas,' she called to him, and he looked around. His face lit up on seeing her and he hurried his step to meet her.

'Tillie, I was just calling on you, and Harriet said you weren't home from work yet.' He desperately wanted to kiss her, but took her hand and kissed it as propriety demanded.

'Ah, that's why you were frowning so. Were you going to lecture me? I'd hate to miss out,' she joked.

'The pleasure of seeing you has made me forget what I was going to say,' he assured her.

'Are you staying for dinner?' she asked.

'No, just dropping in to see you. I don't wish to overstep my welcome.'

'You could not,' Matilda assured him. 'It is odd that you never felt that way until now.'

'The situation has changed,' he said. 'Shall we walk or are you too tired and prefer to go in? I could join you for a drink before departing.'

'I am happy to walk. Allow me to place my bag inside and let Harriet know I am safe,' she said, and Thomas returned with her. Moments later, they exited the household and made their way to the park.

'Thank you,' she said, looking up at him.

'For what?' he asked, surprised, forgetting his gift.

'The beautiful roses, they are breathtaking and very

thoughtful,' she said. 'I think I will put them in my room so I can see them first thing when I awake.'

'Ah, you are most welcome. I'm happy to be thought of first thing.'

'So romantic,' Matilda continued. 'I would not have picked Thomas Ashdown for a romantic.'

'Come on,' he said, looking surprised and hurt. 'I gave you a frog that day by the creek, and I put worms on your fishing line. That's the stuff of poets.'

Matilda laughed. 'Be still my beating heart.'

They walked together in comfortable silence for a few moments, then Matilda looked up at him as she linked her arm through his. 'I was just thinking of you when I saw you,' she said. They moved to allow several cyclists to pass by at a great speed.

'Excellent. What were you thinking?' Thomas asked.

'That I would like to see you,' she said frankly.

Thomas smiled. 'I think that nearly every minute of the day,' he admitted. Then Matilda noticed his frown. 'Why? Is everything all right?' he added, his happy acceptance of having been in her thoughts overcome by foreboding.

She laughed. 'Of course. Am I not allowed to miss you?'

'Please do.'

As they walked, Matilda was conscious of making a better effort than last time when he sought affection from her. She asked. 'Do you not find the situation between us now a little odd? It is hard to know how we should progress, is it not? I want to see you often, but when I do, I am sated for a while and then anxious again. I suspect it is because I worry about you going about your daily work.'

'Imagine how I feel,' he said, 'knowing the situations you put yourself in for your work and that I can't protect you around the clock. Mark my words, if anyone harms you, I will hunt them down.' He stretched his neck, loosening his tie just a little and regaining control.

Matilda pulled closer to him and smiled, delighted. She looked out over the river to admire the boats bobbing in the afternoon tide.

Thinking on her words he asked, 'Do you think in time as we define our new relationship, it will feel more natural than the friendship once did?'

'Yes, I suspect so,' she answered.

'Tell me, Tillie; I want to know what you feel about me and our relationship. Not as a friend of your brother, or as family, or as your current suitor. I want to know how you feel about me in your future.'

Matilda bit her lip and looked straight ahead as she contemplated his question. She wanted to ensure her answer satisfied him and she had expected he would seek clarity when she had been flippant with his affection recently. Her past bout of jealousy over his attentions to the widowed Mrs Sophie Cornish – work-related interest only as it turned out – made her look at Thomas as other women might and she would not make the mistake of leaving him open to affection elsewhere.

Thomas waited.

'I think it is hard for us to know how to act together romantically because of our family history. It feels more awkward, I imagine, than it would if I were to meet you now and you were to ask me out, and we had much to learn about each other.'

'That's true,' Thomas said. 'Do you miss that opportunity?'

'No,' she said quickly enough for his satisfaction. 'We have a greater understanding than new couples and that's comforting.'

'Comforting is not a word that I want you to think of when thinking of me, unless you are on your sick bed and I am caring for you,' he said flatly.

Then Matilda laughed.

'What is it?'

'I have a brilliant idea.'

'Do tell,' he encouraged her.

'No, I shall surprise you. Sometime in the next week, our relationship will change,' she said.

'All right,' he said hesitantly.

'Do not be alarmed,' she said and patted his arm. 'It will be fun, I promise, and I may even steal a kiss or two if I can get away with it.'

He raised her hand to his lips, kissed it, and pulled her as close as he could within the limits of decency. She then saw his troubled expression.

'I should not be expecting a surprise like on my seventh birthday when you and Daniel told me you had bought me a horse and then gave me a wooden toy one, should I?'

Matilda laughed. 'I had forgotten about that.'

'Hmm,' he said. 'I was so excited all day. Or the surprise like the time you wanted to show me the new tree house you had built, which resulted in me standing under a branch looking up while you tipped a bucket of water down on me? Is it the same sort of surprise?' he teased.

'Goodness, I did not realise I was such a terrible child. One wonders why you like me at all?' she grinned up at him.

'Why indeed,' he said, holding her gaze.

'I assure you; it is a professional surprise. That should alleviate your concerns,' Matilda said decisively.

'Good Lord no,' Thomas muttered, and she laughed.

All was well in the world again, Matilda thought, for now.

Chapter 11

The following afternoon on a glorious and bright winter's day, Matilda and Georgina hurried to keep up with the matron as she led them through the sterile hallways of the female wards of the asylum. Not that the matron had a longer stride, but the ladies were curious and wanted to take in as much of the surroundings as they could. The matron, on the other hand, had seen it all and had no time to spare.

'Your editor has assured me that your stories will be sympathetic and that you will also add value while you are here dually reporting and volunteering,' she said.

'Yes, Matron, we are excited by the prospect of being able to be of assistance,' Matilda assured her.

'You understand you are to sign in and remember to sign out of the visitor book every time you enter the premises? That way, if there is an incident, we know if you are on the premises or not.'

'Of course,' Matilda said.

'If you hear the alarm ring or if there is any cause for concern or danger pending, you are to follow the instructions of the nurse or doctor stationed near your area,' she said, issuing instructions as she walked. 'Do not get separated, as we prefer our volunteers to work in pairs.'

'Yes, Matron,' Georgina snapped back, and Matilda restrained a giggle as she glanced at Georgina, expecting her to salute. Georgina made an impish face in return.

They entered a large room where several women sat around in various stages of occupation. Some knitted, a woman painted in the corner near a window where the light was particularly good, and several sat listening as a woman read them a story. Other volunteers – notable by their informal dress – moved among the ladies helping and offering encouragement.

The matron told Matilda and Georgina, 'Not every patient can work, and some are best to work just a few hours a day and then enjoy personal activities rather than overtax themselves. That is where our volunteers can assist with reading, crafts, letter writing, and so on.'

A woman that Matilda guessed was in her forties, with long blonde braided hair and a strong jawline, approached them. When closer, Matilda realised she was much younger, but her worried countenance had added years to her face.

'Do they need help, Matron?' she asked, looking from Matilda to Georgina and back.

'No thank you, Esther, the ladies are here to spend some time with you and the other residents,' the matron said.

Esther touched Georgina's sleeve, feeling the fine fabric of her dress. She then turned her attention to Matilda and said 'pretty'.

Matilda smiled and thanked her, thinking how Esther herself might have been pretty had she a little more weight on her frame and a less stressed look upon her face.

'Ah, you've met Esther then!'

Matilda had to look up at the tall lady with a kindly face that greeted them. She had red hair worn in a bun, a ruddy complexion, and a plain dress with an enormous fabric flower pinned to the front. 'I'm Winifred, the volunteer manager today. Good afternoon, Matron.'

'Good afternoon, Winifred,' the matron said. 'Allow me to introduce Miss Matilda Hayward and Miss Georgina Urry, the two volunteers I spoke with you about. I shall leave them in your capable hands,' she said and, giving all parties a curt nod, departed.

'Thank you for allowing us to participate,' Matilda said.

'Oh no, thank you, Miss Hayward and Miss Urry,' Winifred said.

The ladies insisted Winifred call them by their first name and Winifred reciprocated with the informalities.

'I confess I am a little nervous, Winifred,' Matilda said, noting that Georgina looked quite the opposite – most at home and ready to roll up her sleeves. She berated herself privately for her lack of confidence.

'It's only natural. I too was anxious when I first started here,' Winifred said in a whisper. 'But I assure you, these ladies are all very harmless and gentle souls. They have been here quite some time.'

As one of the patients approached, Winifred said in a louder voice to her two new volunteers: 'I see you are admiring the flower on my dress. Why, here's Birdie, she made it for me.'

Birdie beamed from ear to ear and clasped her hands.

'What talent you have, Birdie,' Georgina said, getting into the spirit of it. 'I'm terrible at sewing but I can draw.'

'Oh, you are the illustrator, wonderful,' Winifred said. 'Let's put you to work, and Matilda, I have just the job for you! I understand you are a writer, and several of the ladies would like to tell the stories of their lives.'

Matilda beamed as big a smile as Birdie.

'That would be my pleasure,' she said, delighted to have a role that would allow her to write some wonderful copy for Mrs Lawson and the *Women's Journal*, and possibly provide some insights as to how the ladies became wards of the asylum.

'Lovely. Shall we begin with Birdie then?' Winifred asked.

Matilda guessed Birdie's name was a term of endearment, given she was such a bird-like creature, but she would later learn otherwise.

*****

A loud wail that seemed to encompass the building was heard and Matilda and several volunteers jumped from their seats.

'Do not be fearful,' Winifred assured them, 'sounds of this nature are quite common and the orderlies will see to it.'

'He's jumped!' Birdie declared, pointing to the window, 'I saw him jump.'

Matilda looked to where Birdie was pointing. A window on the second level of the men's wing was ajar.

'He was flapping his wings, but they did not work,' another patient, Esther, who sat nearby the window knitting, added.

'Ladies, return to your seats now. All will be well.'

Matilda, Georgina and the other volunteer ladies assisted Winifred by getting their groups returned to their crafts and settled. Matilda exchanged a look with Georgina, who looked appropriately surprised.

As Winifred approached, Matilda asked, 'Does that happen often?'

'No. But it does happen,' she whispered. 'Along with drownings, hangings, and other terrible deaths. Perils of the place, I'm afraid.'

Matilda nodded and subtly watched through the window as two men in suits whom she assumed to be in charge – doctors – studied the victim's prone form. The orderlies herded patients from the scene and then, twenty minutes later or so, she saw Thomas arrive with Detective Dart and several police officers in uniform. She loved watching Thomas in action as he studied the scene and directed his men. Detective Dart was talking to the doctor, who looked to be the senior. Then Matilda recognised a member of the press who had just arrived.

Matilda suggested Birdie take a break from sharing her story and return to her craft, which she most happily accepted given the story seemed to have stalled and gone around in a circle. Matilda said quietly to Georgina. 'I see a journalist is in attendance. I too am going to seek the story.

If I don't come back before the end of our shift, I'll meet you outside.'

'Good for you,' Georgina said, encouraging her.

Matilda excused herself to Winifred and headed outdoors. She remembered the journalist – he was of medium height, mid-20s, a boyish face with foppish hair that needed a cut – they had briefly met once before in the Botanic Gardens when an artist was murdered, his body left against a tree. The journalist nodded a greeting on seeing her and smiled.

'You didn't take long to get here,' he said.

'I happened to be on hand, volunteering,' Matilda said.

'Ah. See anything?' he asked.

'Maybe,' she said and then smiled, seeing his keen expression. 'No, I just heard the reaction.'

He grinned and offered his hand. 'Robert Winrow, *Brisbane Courier*,' he said by way of introduction.

'Matilda Hayward, the *Women's Journal*. My illustrator Miss Urry is also inside volunteering,' she said.

Matilda saw Thomas glance her way. His expression conveyed confusion as to her presence and his glance to the journalist beside her did not go unnoticed. He returned his attention to the crime scene.

Matilda and Robert turned to look as a hansom cab pulled up and a man with a cane alighted.

'That's the coroner,' Robert said. 'I'd love to get a word with him or the detectives.'

'Me too,' Matilda said, not letting on about her relationship.

'The older guy is a softie but the young guy, Detective Ashdown, is surly,' the journalist informed her.

'Hmm, is that so?' Matilda mused.

'Yeah, he's their top gun, I've heard. Solved every case that's landed in his lap,' Robert said, 'but he could do with a stint at charm school.'

'I imagine if the police need us to disseminate some information to the community, then they are more charming as required,' Matilda said, adding what she had heard from other writers, but pleased to hear the summary of Thomas's worth.

They stood watching and soon the scene was cleared as if it had never happened, except for Thomas and Detective Dart who lingered and were talking to the coroner. Matilda was keen to catch Thomas, and it was just the time and opportunity to put her plan into action. Finally, he approached the press party of two.

'Detective, can you tell us anything about what happened today?' Robert asked generously, including Matilda. He most likely would not have done so if she were a man.

'Good afternoon, Mr Winrow,' Thomas acknowledged Robert, then turned his attention to Matilda.

'Good afternoon, Detective. I am Matilda Hayward from the *Women's Journal.*'

Thomas realised the game and smiled. Several orderlies passed by, and Thomas gave a small bow to her.

'Detective Thomas Ashdown, at your service. I suggest this is not a place for a lady,' he said.

'Yes, most men would suggest that, Detective, but nevertheless, here I am.' She held his gaze. 'As my colleague said, could you provide a quote on what happened this afternoon for our reports?' she asked, keeping a very serious face and studying him. 'I believe the man fell from that window?' Matilda indicated the window on the second level of the large grey building opposite.

'Did you see it?' Thomas asked quickly.

'No, only the aftermath.'

'In the aftermath, did you see anyone in the window or running from the scene?' Thomas asked.

'No, I did not, and I was hoping to ask the questions,' Matilda said with a small smile.

Thomas restrained a smile and said, 'I cannot comment on the incident or victim as I am yet to receive the coroner's findings, Miss Hayward, was it?'

'Am I that forgettable, Detective Ashdown, or is detail not your strength?' she asked.

Robert chuckled beside her.

'Given you are probably the most unforgettable young lady I have ever seen, I shall wear the blame for lack of attention to detail,' he said. 'You, on the other hand, Mr Winrow, are most memorable from your last story – or should I call it fiction piece – that you constructed for the *Courier*.'

'I hope it helped your case,' Robert said facetiously, knowing full well it did not.

'It would help if you got your facts right,' Thomas snapped back.

'Then give us something,' Robert pushed him.

'A male patient has fallen from a second-floor window at the Wacol Asylum for the Insane. Time of death an hour ago. The patient was aged in his forties.' With a curt bow to Matilda, Thomas turned and retreated to Detective Dart's side. He did not get far before Matilda called to him.

'Detective, one more quick thing please.'

Thomas, hiding a smile, returned.

'Miss Hayward?'

'As I assume that gentleman talking to Detective Dart is the coroner – did he give you an indication of the cause of death other than the obvious fall… such as narcotics, evidence of a struggle or so forth?' Matilda asked and saw Thomas's eyes widen. Robert made an appreciative sound beside her.

Thomas cleared his throat. 'At this stage, there appears to be no suspicious circumstances, but I won't rule anything out until I get the coroner's report.'

Thomas again gave a small nod and returned to Detective Dart.

'Well, I suspect that's as good as we'll get,' Robert said. 'Nice work.'

'Thank you,' Matilda said. 'Good to see you again.'

'See you next story,' he said with a wink and departed. She watched him walk away and then turning, abandoned her post to go meet with Georgina.

Entering the room, she found the volunteers' shift was just winding up, and thanking the manager, Winifred, the two ladies departed. They did not speak until they were further down the hallway.

'Are you all right? That was unexpected,' Georgina said and exhaled.

'Gruesome, but I am fine, thank you,' Matilda assured her. 'Let's catch up with the detectives and find out what really happened. If they'll tell us. Thomas was very cloak and dagger given the *Brisbane Courier* journalist was beside me.'

'You can't blame him,' Georgina said. 'It is a daily paper and people are easily panicked in the city.'

Matilda gave her a look of surprise… that was an angle worth pursuing. Were country folk more resilient to crisis and drama? They ventured to the asylum's front apron and stairs and saw the man with the cane – the coroner – talking with Thomas at the hansom cab. Detective Dart saw the two ladies and approached.

'Miss Hayward, Miss Urry, how delightful,' Harry said with a small bow.

The three exchanged greetings, and walking ahead, Georgina beamed at Detective Dart. 'Last time we met, Detective, it was at the art gallery,' Georgina said. 'That awful first exhibition by Mr Marlon Dominey. This is indeed a different scene,' she said and descended the stairs to talk with him some feet away.

As Matilda waited for Thomas, a man appeared through the door behind Matilda – an orderly dressed in the uniform of white pants and top. He was tall, blond, and strikingly handsome.

'Miss, may I be of assistance?' he asked and gave a small bow. 'Nikolaus Derichs at your service.'

Matilda turned to greet him. 'Mr Derichs, thank you, but I am a volunteer and just departing for the day.'

'Ah, that is kind of you to volunteer your time. May I know your name?' he asked with a smile.

'Matilda Hayward, Miss,' she said. 'Is that a German accent I hear?'

'Yes, my family moved here, well, to Mount Alford, not too far from here. Many Germans are settling there, but I came to the city for work.'

Before Matilda could reply, Thomas appeared at the bottom of the stairs and nipped the introduction in the bud.

'Miss Hayward, allow me to see you and Miss Urry off the premises,' he said with a nod to the orderly. She noted his eyes narrowing at the man beside her.

'Of course, Detective, that would be appreciated.' She turned to Mr Derichs beside her and said, 'Please excuse me.' Matilda accepted Thomas's hand down the stairs and joined Detective Dart and Georgina as they walked up the path of the asylum to hail their rides.

'Do you know that man?' Thomas asked.

'No, he was just offering to assist me,' she said.

'I'm sure he was,' Thomas muttered, with a glance backwards. He turned his attention to Matilda and smiled. 'So, I am not good at remembering detail?'

She laughed. 'I told you I would come up with an interesting way for us to re-meet. Strangers, in the professional sense. It will keep us on our toes,' she teased him. 'You looked terribly handsome studying the scene of the crime.'

He grinned. 'Is that so? And to think I have wasted my previous crimes scenes on the dead when I was looking so appealing.'

'That's a good thing, thank you very much,' Matilda assured him. 'I hardly need competition for your attentions. So, you are not a fan of the *Brisbane Courier's* Mr Winrow?'

Thomas grimaced. 'Pretentious rabble-rouser. You don't win favours by writing stories that do nothing to assist us and are outright fearmongering. He will get nothing from me till hell freezes over.'

'And what about that other journalist?' Matilda asked.

Thomas frowned. 'Was it Miss Hayward? She asked all the right questions but I'm a little sketchy on detail…'

Matilda laughed and playfully hit his arm. As they caught up with Detective Dart and Georgina, Matilda resisted the urge to loop her arm through his as she kept up their professional front. She was enjoying seeing him in his work capacity.

Thomas looked down at her with affection. 'I finally get you away from the freak show and unstable artists, and now you are going to regularly visit an asylum.' He shook his head in disbelief.

'Yes, and I can't wait. Not that I'm excited to see people's misery, of course,' she added quickly. 'But maybe my stories will enlighten readers and then women like Mrs Hilda Rodgers won't suffer unnecessarily. Maybe they will make us all more sympathetic to those less fortunate.'

'And maybe they'll sell more papers,' Thomas added cynically.

Matilda sighed and turned to Detective Dart. 'Thomas is such a wet blanket. Do you not think he needs some cheering up, Detective Dart?'

'It would be hard not to become cynical in your line of work, detectives,' Georgina added. 'I know from my work, some days I could just snap a pencil with the sheer frustration of it.'

Matilda could not help smiling, comparing their lives with that of the men in their company. The frustrations usually came from men in the first instance, but that discussion was for another time.

'You might be right, Miss Hayward and Miss Urry,' Detective Dart said, adopting a thoughtful look. 'Thomas, you need some cheering up and are becoming far too cynical about your work. Perhaps you need to stop investigating murder for a while.'

'Well, if the city could stop producing murder victims, I may just get a break,' Thomas retorted. But then he mellowed. 'The ladies of the *Women's Journal* are right of course. I'll try to see the bright side, like your current role of reporting at the asylum, Matilda. Such fun,' he said with a smile, and made Georgina and Harry chuckle.

'Now you are just making fun of me,' she said with a wry look.

As the omnibus arrived, the party of four took the ride to a central location before each departing for their respective homes for the evening. Matilda happily accepted the opportunity to be walked home by Thomas.

'Is it true what you said today… that there might not be any suspicious circumstances related to the man who fell?' Matilda asked.

'Jumped more likely,' Thomas said, 'but in strict

confidence, he had the smell of a drug about him. Percy Sturgess was his name, married, no children. The coroner will confirm what the drug is, but I have my suspicions.'

'Hmm. He's not Elijah's patient, thank goodness. Did you find out anything about Mrs Hilda Rodgers?' she asked.

'Yes.'

Matilda looked up at Thomas and he raised an eyebrow in her direction.

'No, I'm not telling you.'

'But why not? We probably know more than you from what we have discussed and discovered at the *Women's Journal* and from our volunteering today,' she said.

'I am aware of your game, Matilda. I know you are trying to entice me to give you details by bartering.' He narrowed his eyes and regarded her with suspicion. 'All right then, I shall share as long as you do the same and do not publish my information.'

'Never. Without your consent. Unless I already knew it, of course,' Matilda said, adding provisos as they came to her. 'Go ahead.'

Thomas told of meeting with Mrs Hilda Rodgers' sons, husband, and cousin Flora, and of his impressions. When he finished, Matilda said, 'Goodness, you were right, we had none of that information.'

Thomas's eyes widened, and he was about to issue his warning again when she laughed. He narrowed his eyes at her. 'I need to work out when you are teasing me, so I'm prepared in advance.'

'One would have thought after all these years you might

have developed that skill,' she said. 'But as I recall, you always were easy to trap.'

'Not by everyone, trust me. Just by a certain person who always held my heart in her hands,' Thomas said, raising her hand to his lips as they took the path to her home.

'Yes perhaps,' she said with a smile. 'It did work to my advantage a few times. Remember when you and Daniel made the raft, and we took it out for the first time on the creek.'

'Yes,' he said drily, knowing what was coming.

Matilda laughed and squeezed his arm. 'My hero.'

'You could have told me you could swim before I jumped in to save you. I was wondering why Daniel was so nonchalant as you splashed around in front of him.'

'You got me back enough times,' she assured him.

'None come to mind,' Thomas said. 'But don't dodge the subject. Tell me, what you know then.'

'From our discussion at the *Women's Journal*, those ladies who met Mrs Rodgers, like Betty, our deputy editor, are convinced she was as sane as the day was long.'

Thomas nodded. 'It appears everyone I've spoken to except her husband agrees.'

'What is quite odd though, is that several of the ladies in residence that I met at the asylum today are all rather fixated on flying. I mentioned this to Elijah, and he said he had a patient who complained of back pain because her wings were growing.'

'And that would be why they are in there, I suspect,' Thomas said.

'I wonder if it is because they are restrained,' Matilda mused. 'I don't mean they are tied up, but there are large fences around the grounds, there are locks on doors and alarms everywhere. Does the mind naturally go to escape and flying?'

'It's as good an analysis as any, I guess. I was told today by a hospital nurse that it was also Mrs Rodgers' last thought before dying – to fly.'

'No?' Matilda's eyes widened.

'That is strictly between us,' he said, a warning tone to his voice.

'Unless I should ask the nurse myself as part of our story and investigation,' she said.

'Then publish her name so it is legitimately from her, and I am not your source.'

'Aye, aye, Captain, or rather, Detective,' Matilda teased him again, and he shook his head at her. 'So, what will you do about Mrs Rodgers' death now?'

'I have a few more lines of enquiry, but I fear there is nothing more to go on,' Thomas said. 'She jumped. The marks around her wrist were my only real cause for suspicion, but I suspect there may be no case to answer for and the coroner will rule it a suicide. Besides, I have cases piling up so I cannot spend too much more time on Mrs Rodgers' file with nothing but dead ends, so to speak.'

'Then you must decide who to believe.'

'I don't believe the husband for a moment,' Thomas said.

'I shouldn't tell you this, but since we are trading information...'

'Go on,' Thomas encouraged her.

'Elijah asked his boss if he remembered Mrs Rodgers and what his thoughts were on her.'

Thomas's eyes widened with interest. 'That's useful. What did he say?'

'In Elijah's words, his boss declared Mrs Rodgers mad as the day is long and believed she should not have been released.'

'Hmm,' Thomas said as he mulled over Matilda's comment. 'My gut tells me something is amiss, but I can find no proof to confirm it.'

'Yet,' Matilda agreed. 'I hope you do not give up on this, Thomas. I know you may not have a choice, but I feel the same as you. Something is afoot.'

Chapter 12

Elijah stopped and waited as he saw his sister, Matilda, entering the grounds of the asylum, another woman in her company. He had been doing the rounds and had stepped outside to enjoy a cup of tea and some fresh air during his late morning break. The grounds were beautiful, best when the asylum was at your back and not in view.

The woman was a good head taller than Matilda and handsome in her own way, if not a little ungainly – she walked with purpose and not with the airs and graces some women display. She openly laughed at something Matilda said without fear of appearing unladylike. Quite the opposite of Miss Lily Chappell. The woman lacked the polish of his sister. Perhaps that was it, he thought, studying them. The thought was surprising given Matilda grew up in a household full of males; she should be more like her companion, truth be known.

'Elijah!' Matilda called, waving and smiling at seeing him. The two women hurried their steps. 'How delightful and how handsome you look.'

Elijah laughed. Matilda was always surprising him. 'Thank you. May I say the same of both of you ladies on this beautiful morning?' he said with sincerity.

'You may!' Matilda smiled. 'Allow me to introduce Miss Georgina Urry, a most talented illustrator from the *Women's Journal*.' She turned to Georgina and added, 'this is my brother, Dr Elijah Hayward.'

'Ah yes, I see. No family resemblance,' Georgina said, and they both laughed. Elijah gave a small bow.

'Lovely to meet you, Miss Urry,' he said.

'Please, call me Georgina. Or George, if you prefer, but nobody seems to. So, you've just started here, your sister tells me?' Georgina asked as they joined him on the open apron area outside the asylum doors.

'Yes, my first week. Interesting to say the least,' he said.

'I imagine. I hear they are all mad,' Georgina said in a hushed voice. Elijah laughed again.

'I wouldn't like to spoil the ending, but yes, it is true,' he added.

Georgina grinned. 'Well, good for you, Dr Hayward. This will give you some interesting experience on your written work record.'

'Exactly Miss Urry, that is just what I thought.' He ignored the request to call her by her Christian name in the work environment. 'Maybe next I'll work as a coroner and round off the full life journey.'

'At least the patients would not answer back,' Georgina said.

'And they'd always be dying to see me,' he retorted with

a grin, bringing on another round of laughs from the ladies. Elijah felt Matilda looking at him with a surprised expression. It was not that he didn't have a personality, it was just that he rarely showed it or needed to when in the company of his rowdy family and in particular, his twin brother, Gideon.

'Best we get to our volunteer work, then,' Matilda said, 'in case we get mistaken for patients.'

'Every chance,' Elijah said and gave his sister a nudge. 'Lovely to meet you, Miss Urry, I'm sure I shall see you around.'

'But not around the bend,' Georgina retorted and laughed as she hitched her arm through Matilda's and they ventured through the doors of the asylum, Elijah watching them as they depart. He considered Miss Urry to be the most interesting woman he had met for some time – she did not swoon, nor did she bat her eyelashes once, nor be coy. How refreshing.

*****

The young constable dashed down the hallway of the Roma Street Police Headquarters, coming to a halt outside Detective Thomas Ashdown's office. Thomas was studying the board while Harry wrote up notes about their case – a case that they both conceded they must close.

'Sirs?' the young man said breathlessly, leaning into the office.

'What is it, Constable?' Thomas asked.

'There's been a murder. An old man, living at Bowen Hills on Jordan Terrace… his house steward asked that you come quickly.'

Thomas turned to Harry. 'Jordan Terrace… it couldn't be, could it?'

Harry shook his head with dismay. 'I just hope none of those Rodgers boys has gone and done something stupid.'

The constable gave Thomas the house number as Harry went to retrieve his hat and coat.

'Take a colleague and go to secure the scene, Constable, as quickly as you can. I'll notify the coroner and be there directly,' Thomas instructed.

As Harry joined him, Thomas showed him the house number, confirming their suspicions – the death was at the premises of Mr Raymond Rodgers – Hilda's husband. Whether it was him remained to be seen – to the constable's eyes, the definition of old could be anyone in or beyond their third decade of life.

'We've got grounds to keep the case open now, I'd say,' Harry said as they departed with a detour to the coroner's office.

They soon alighted out the front of Mr Raymond Rodgers's mansion for the second time that week. They passed the constable on the gate.

'The deceased has been laid out on the veranda, sir. I believe he has been moved,' the constable informed them.

'For the love of God,' Thomas muttered impatiently and shook his head as they made their way to the front entrance. Before them, lying flat out with a sheet covering all but his face was Mr Raymond Rodgers. Nearby, three staff members stood staring – two housekeepers in various states of shock and disbelief – and the house steward they had met previously. All three were effectively now unemployed and suspects. The house steward stepped forward to speak with the detectives.

'Is this how you found him?' Thomas asked impatiently.

Harry stepped in and, with a quick grab to Thomas's shoulder, deflected him to the body. Thomas frowned, understanding his partner's motive, but for the love of God, why would you move the body?

'Ladies, step inside if you will, please,' Harry said, directing them. 'We'll have a constable come and get a statement from you both shortly.'

Thomas nudged the young constable standing by the corpse. 'That'll be you, Constable. Get as much detail as you can about where they were and what they saw.'

'Yes, sir,' he said and left Thomas alone with the corpse.

The house steward joined them and said, 'Mr Rodgers was lying down there on the path, beaten in a most undignified manner. I managed to bring him here and cover him.'

Thomas reined in his anger and said nothing, his jaw locked with frustration. He ran a finger between his neck and necktie, releasing his discomfort.

Harry continued to play the diplomat.

'I understand your concern and it was very loyal of you,' Harry said. 'But for future reference, it is best not to touch a crime scene for fear you are incriminated in it, or you accidentally destroy evidence that might assist us in finding the culprit.'

'Me? Incriminated?' the house steward said, losing some of his haughtiness, and replacing it with fear as he looked from Thomas to Harry.

'Can you show me where you found him?' Harry asked.

Thomas exchanged a frustrated glance with Harry, who headed down the path following the house steward. He returned his attention to the corpse, but not for long before he heard the click of a cane and looked up to see the coroner had arrived at the gates. He removed the sheet and studied the body as Dr Nevins joined him.

'Well, that will kill you,' Dr Nevins said, noting the savage blow to the skull.

'Yes indeed,' Thomas said and glanced around hoping to find the object that might have served as a murder weapon.

Dr Nevins knelt. 'He's not been dead long, he's still relatively warm to touch and rigor mortis has not set in.'

Thomas excused himself and left the doctor to do his inspection. He headed down the path. 'Did you see anyone at all?' he asked the house steward.

'Not a soul,' he answered. 'Mr Rodgers was heading out for his post-lunch walk, which he did every day since taking his retirement from work. I did not see him off as he did not require me to organise the carriage or his coat.'

'Has anyone visited today?' Thomas asked.

'No one today which is not unusual. Mr Rodgers rarely entertained or had visitors.'

'Including his sons? No sign of them today?'

'No. They would never willingly come here.' The steward cleared his throat and added, 'It was not a harmonious relationship between father and sons.'

Thomas thanked him and moved around the area where the body was found while Harry escorted the steward back to the house and talked with the coroner. He could find no obvious shoe prints, nothing that would serve as a weapon, and any blood that was there was scuffled as the steward had dragged Mr Rodgers back to the house. Thomas squatted down and studied the area, and then he saw something glint in the sunlight. He rose and moved to the edge of the path and, pulling out his handkerchief, he used it to retrieve a small medicinal dropper bottle. He gave it a slight shake, holding it up to the light and found but an inch of fluid remained in the bottle's bottom. Thomas removed the lid and was quickly accosted by a bitter smell – laudanum. It was the second time he had encountered the smell in two days. It was also on the breath of the jumper from the asylum.

But why did Mr Rodgers have laudanum on him, or did the killer drop the bottle?

Chapter 13

Fourteen patients were occupied in various industries when Matilda and Georgina entered the volunteers' room. It was a sunny room with a high ceiling and minimal furniture placed around the area. One might have forgotten it was an asylum except for the patients all dressed in the same manner and the bars on the windows.

'Ah, here's our two lovely new ladies returned to spend time with us again!' Winifred, the volunteer manager, exclaimed.

'We are very pleased to be back, aren't we, Georgina?' Matilda said, smiling at Winifred and greeting the other volunteers and patients.

'My word we are,' Georgina added. 'I'm keen to see how some of my brilliant art students are doing.'

Birdie approached Matilda and shook her head. 'I am sorry I cannot finish my story with you today,' the skittish woman said, 'but I'm in the middle of painting.'

Matilda glanced at the childlike painting on the easel. 'Oh my, well, I wouldn't want to keep you from that. We'll continue another time, shall we?'

'Let's have a look then,' Georgina said and headed over to Birdie's easel to see the work in progress. Matilda noticed some very fine paintings were works in progress, but Birdie's was not one of them. She felt a small tap on her shoulder and turned to see the Irish lady, Hannah, nearby. She had seen her last session, but they had not spoken.

'I would like my story to be written. Perhaps my children might want to know the truth of it,' Hannah said, moving closer to Matilda than comfort allowed.

'You remember, Hannah, don't you, Matilda?' Winifred asked, coming between them. Everyone was on a first-name basis in the room. It was easier that way.

'Of course. I would love to help you record your story. How many children do you have?' Matilda asked with a glance at Winifred. Some questions were best asked with caution, and Winifred gave her a reassuring nod.

'Four. They be all adults now, and living all over the world. I like most of them,' Hannah said and made Matilda laugh.

'Well, that's a good thing. Let's sit and begin,' Matilda said, inviting Hannah to join her and the two ladies moved to the far side of the room near the windows, where they could enjoy the warm winter sun. 'Have you hurt your arm?'

'Aye,' Hannah patted the bandage on her arm. 'I tripped and fell in the garden. Dr Hayward said it is getting better.' She leaned in, conspiratorially, unaware of the relationship between Matilda and Dr Hayward. 'He has a sweetheart. It's not yer, is it?'

Matilda's eyes widened in surprise. She was just about to

deny he did and then realised why Elijah may have thought it best to say he was courting.

'No, definitely not me. She would be a lucky lady.'

'Lucky lady,' Hannah agreed and nodded. 'Two people shorten the road.'

Matilda smiled. 'Well, that's a lovely saying. Irish, is it?'

'My ma used to say it all the time. Shall I begin my tale?' she asked, folding her hands neatly in her lap.

'Please,' Matilda agreed. Soon she would find out that Hannah's four children never outgrew their childhood, and the husband was now buried in the city cemetery.

*****

Women's Journal
Tuesday, 10 July 1888
Fortnightly edition Vol.1, No.18.
Price, 3d.

Hannah of the asylum

A short series presenting an exclusive insight into life for women at the Asylum for the Insane at Wacol. Report by Matilda Hayward. Illustration by Georgina Urry.

--oOo--

There was much excitement in Hannah's family when they decided to become new Australians and leave their Irish life behind. Her parents, Patrick and Elizabeth, wept at the docks as they waved goodbye to their daughter, her husband of nine years, Mr Edmund Sullivan – a bootmaker, and four young grandchildren – Roisin, 8, Danny, 6 Francis, 5, and Martin, 3.

While the adventure at sea might sound romantic, it was far from it – a long, perilous journey to the unknown to begin a new life in a new country.

'We were so ill,' Hannah said. 'The storms would last forever, and we'd be praying to God that we would make it to land safely.'

Hannah described how the water would sweep over the decks, and they feared the ship would go under.

'My husband, Edmund, rushed out of our cabin many a time to see if we needed to abandon ship. The children would be crying, and I knew my face was as pale as death, but I kept praying.

'One night Edmund had to help all the other men bail water out of the saloon. It was frightening indeed.'

Hannah recalled how the doctor could offer nothing to help the passengers in their state of seasickness.

'My little ones were ailing, we all were, but there was nothing to be done for it. The ship rolled frightfully all day and all night, and we barely saw the light of day for lying below trying to not retch what little we had left in our bellies.'

Last month past, Hannah attained her 55th birthday. The journey of 25 years ago is forgotten most days and what memories she has have been reinvented.

To hear the small Irish woman with a handsome face, speak of her children, you would learn that they are all adults living in different places around the world. Her husband, whom she calls her sweetheart, died after the journey.

The truth is harder to hear. Her children died one after another on that very voyage, and like a dozen or more passengers on that fateful journey, were buried at sea.

Hannah and her husband arrived to begin their new life with nothing but their luggage and each other. Hannah was taken ill and broke down. She blamed her husband, Mr Edmund Sullivan, who wanted to take the journey, for the fate that befell them all. One evening, when she brought him his tea, Hannah laced it with arsenic and murdered her sweetheart. She told the judge she had to sacrifice her husband to the other side so he could provide for their children.

Today, Hannah has no family but receives care from the dedicated workers and volunteers at the asylum. She is a keen gardener and is industrious most days in the asylum grounds or in artistic occupations. Hannah asked me to write to one of her children and so we began that letter which will never be sent or received.

Chapter 14

Wednesday evening drinks and dinner was becoming an institution at Thomas's place of abode. It was an open invitation to any of the men in their circle and Teddy would cook the boys up a storm, the men would have a few drinks, eat well, enjoy a cigar and port, post-dinner, and sometimes even break out the cards. It was a fine mid-week wind down, and no ladies allowed – a replacement for the clubs that a man courting or married was best to avoid. On a couple of occasions, Thomas's partner, Harry, stayed for a drink then headed home to Mrs Dart, and even Mr Hayward had looked in once or twice but never lingered longer than a drink or two – leaving his boys and future son-in-law to let down their hair. Besides, he occasionally liked to take his pipe and frequent his own club.

Tonight's roll call included Thomas, his live-in nephew and chef, Teddy, along with Daniel, Elijah and a friend of Teddy's – Joseph Fieldhouse – who was most popular for bringing expensive, imported Pioneer Golden Flake cigars

– a treat indeed and possibly procured through confiscated contraband in his workplace. Best not to ask. Tonight, Teddy had cooked up a couple of hearty shepherd's pies and on a cool winter's night, the aroma was most welcoming.

'An Irish recipe,' Teddy said, as Thomas appreciated his efforts and poured the men present an ale. They removed themselves to the drawing room, which was in a better condition since Teddy moved in and did a few renovations while waiting to secure a job.

'Smells great. Do the prisoners get food that good?' Daniel asked Teddy.

'On our watch they do,' he said with a grin at Joseph. 'It's a funny place to work – don't get me wrong, I'm grateful to your Aunt Audrey for securing me a chance to finish my apprenticeship.'

'She's got her fingers in a lot of civic pies,' Elijah said. 'When she was determined to get you a placement, we feared where you'd end up,' he said with a grin. 'So, what's it like, the prison?'

'It's home to some, hell to others,' Teddy said with a glance at Joseph, who nodded his agreement. 'They'll complain about the food just because they can, but if they were released, half of them wouldn't get a meal every day, living on the streets, and the other half would be lucky to afford the cuts they get.'

Joseph chuckled. 'A few of the boys who are in for theft said we cook better than their missuses.'

Thomas laughed. 'That might help us get criminals off the street. Can you do a weekly menu, and we'll distribute it in the seedy areas? All confessions welcome.'

'They'll be handing themselves in,' Teddy said, and the men laughed at the idea. 'What's the food like at the madhouse, Elijah?'

'From what I've seen, pretty good if it's not on the wall or being thrown at me,' he joked.

Thomas refrained from mentioning the laudanum that the coroner said was ingested by the recent jumper at the asylum but addressed Elijah when the conversation broke into small groups.

'I don't want to make you work for your dinner, but we found a dropper bottle at the death scene of Mr Raymond Rodgers – it had laudanum in it. I'm yet to know if laudanum was in his blood, but what would a respectable gent be doing with it?'

'Raymond Rodgers? Would he be the husband of the recent jumper?' Elijah asked.

'The very same,' Thomas said.

'Pleasure and pain,' Elijah answered. 'It dulls pain but is highly addictive and can bring on euphoria, followed by debilitating lows. These days it can only be administered by a chemist or doctor.' Elijah studied Thomas. 'I know where you are going with this. You're thinking Mr Rodgers didn't have it for his own needs… he had it for the purpose of keeping his wife unstable?'

Thomas nodded. 'Exactly. I know you've only been at the asylum for a week, but have you got any feedback about Hilda Rodgers?' He honoured Matilda's wishes and did not mention that she had tipped him off, besides, he was keen to hear it directly from Elijah.

'My boss, Dr Stephen O'Shea, thinks she was insane. Mind you, he's got some quite extreme views,' Elijah said.

'Such as?' Daniel tuned into their conversation and prompted his younger brother.

Elijah soon held court with the men.

'Well, for this group's ears only, he believes hysteria in women is due to several factors. He believes a woman who is not a wife and mother is fundamentally unable to function within society's expectations of her and thus, would inevitably wind up in an asylum.'

'Good grief,' Daniel said. 'We'd better warn our spinster aunts and widowed friends to get hitched as soon as possible. I'd love to hear Aunt Audrey's opinion on that.'

The men chuckled.

'He's very congenial. He might even talk Aunt Audrey around to his way of thinking,' Elijah said in jest.

'What else does this doctor believe?' Thomas encouraged Elijah as he reached for the opened bottle in their midst and topped up the party.

Elijah reddened slightly and then said, 'He believes if the ladies eat too much flesh – mainly red meat – it induces masturbation.'

All the men looked surprised, and Thomas refrained from responding. Once he and Daniel would have had plenty to say on that topic, but now that he was courting Matilda, any comments might reflect on his present thoughts and actions. He did the best thing he could think to do and said nothing.

'Does that work both ways?' Teddy asked. 'Because Joe and I serve meat to the prison boys every day.'

'They are probably all in their cells feeling very frustrated, if that's the case,' Joseph said with a laugh.

'I'm not sure it applies to either sex,' Elijah said. 'I can't say I've come across a study that proves that to be the case. He also believes female exercise should be tied to domestic chores to provide true satisfaction.'

On this one, Thomas laughed, and Daniel snorted.

'I must share that one with Matilda,' Daniel said. He nudged Thomas. 'I'll tell her she'd best get in and help Harriet around the house or she will never feel complete.'

Thomas grinned. 'So, this doctor is sane, is he?' he asked.

'Debatable, I guess,' Elijah said with a smile. 'I have had little time with my counterpart yet, Victor McQuade. He's fairly aloof, so I don't know if he agrees with Dr O'Shea or not.' Elijah returned to Thomas's investigation. 'What's the next step with the medicine bottle?'

'The coroner is testing if Mr Rodgers had laudanum in his system at the time of his death. We may need to do the same for Mrs Rodgers.'

'They have buried her, haven't they?' Teddy asked. 'I saw it in the newspaper.'

'Yep, we'll have to dig her up,' Thomas said unceremoniously. 'If one or both of them have it in their systems, I'll be trying to find who prescribed the drug to them.'

'And if they both don't have laudanum in their bodies?' Daniel asked Thomas.

'Then the bottle likely belongs to the killer, I suspect.'

*****

Matilda was so rarely home alone that she found the concept both exciting and frightening. Cook and Harriet had departed early on Matilda's assurance that she could help herself to the plate left out for her with no assistance, her father was at his club for just a few hours he assured her, despite Matilda's insistence to enjoy himself and not rush home. Gideon was nowhere to be seen and Thomas, Elijah and Daniel were all at the boys' night. The fire was lit, the room was cosy, and she stood momentarily, not sure what to do.

'I shall have dinner first,' she declared out loud to no one. 'Then I will do some research on asylums and women's constitutions. I may be able to draw some conclusions for my next article… Elijah might check them for me. Pa must have something useful in his library.'

She ventured to the kitchen to retrieve the plate Cook had prepared for her and thought about the future and brightened, as she had a brilliant idea.

When I am married to Thomas, she stopped at the thought… it was the first time she had said those words even to herself, but she found the concept most exciting. She continued her train of thought… when I am married to Thomas, I shall have a girls' gathering on the night that he has his men's dinner. Pa will allow me to have it here, I am sure, so Thomas can maintain his tradition at his home. I shall invite all my sisters-in-law. She laughed at the idea and considered the candidates for her brothers' hands in marriage.

Minnie has already captured Amos's heart and hand.

With luck, Alice will be Mrs Daniel Hayward.

Could this new lady – Miss Lily Chappell – win Gideon's heart?

As for Elijah, sweet, clever, caring Elijah… who knows.

The front door burst open, and Matilda hurried from the kitchen to the hallway.

'Aunt Audrey!'

'Matilda, dear, terrible news. I must break it to Mary,' she said, all harried.

'She has gone for the day, Aunt. What has happened? Are you all right?'

'Yes, I am fine, but the Exhibition Building has burned to the ground!'

'No, that grand building! Is it not full of theatre costumes, plants and a skating rink as well?'

'Yes, tragic. Gone up in flames right to the roof. They were experimenting with electric light for that wretched skating rink and now look what has happened. There will be no competition this year.' Aunt Audrey shook her head.

'Perhaps I'd better go and see if I can write something from witnesses' accounts or talk with the fire brigade on hand,' Matilda said.

'Absolutely not. They will send you away immediately,' Aunt Audrey scolded. 'The scene is most dangerous. I could see the flames on my way here, and the smoke was thick across Fortitude Valley and the city centre. Plus, with this breeze blowing, it will take some effort for our poor firemen to get it under control. I think I need a cup of tea.'

'Of course, Aunt, do give me your coat and hat and come sit by the fire. Fear not, I am quite adept at making tea and Cook has some cake on hand for fortitude.'

'Thank you, my dear.' Aunt Audrey sighed. 'I do hope no one was injured.'

'It would be the perfect opportunity to hide a body,' Matilda mused and on hearing Aunt Audrey's gasp, realised she had said that aloud. Maybe she was lucky that Thomas had revealed his affection for her, she thought. How many other men might tolerate her strange predilection for drama?

Chapter 15

The coroner welcomed the two detectives as they entered his room the next morning. As always, the smell accosted Thomas more so than his partner. Harry pulled his coat closer around him.

'Chillier in here than it is outside, Patrick,' he said with a shiver.

'Keeps me and the corpses preserved,' Dr Nevins joked, dressed in only a light coat jacket. 'I've got good news if you are hoping for a clue, bad news if you are trying to solve a case.' He elicited a groan from both men.

'If we go out and come back in, will it change anything?' Thomas joked.

Dr Nevins laughed. 'Cheer up, it could be worse. It could be you on the slab with me standing over you with a scalpel. I promise I'd be gentle.'

Thomas grimaced. 'Should that day ever occur, just be quick! The sooner I get in the ground the better.'

'It is the stuff of nightmares,' Harry agreed. 'What have you got, Doc?'

'The bad news is that there is not a drop of laudanum in Mr Rodgers' body. So, it is unlikely that the bottle of laudanum belongs to him.'

'Damn,' Thomas said and sighed. 'Given Mrs Hilda Rodgers had been dead for days before he died, it's unlikely he would be carrying the laudanum around to inflict it on her. But not impossible if he forgot to remove it from his coat.'

'What was the good news?' Harry asked.

'If you find it in Mrs Rodgers' body, then you can make sense of why a woman who worked so hard to be free took her own life once she had won that freedom.'

'True,' Thomas said, 'and we have found nothing to the contrary that says she did not take her own life.'

Dr Nevins continued. 'You will be wanting to exhume Mrs Rodgers now, I'm guessing? But be warned, it may be hard to detect anything – time makes a difference. Plus, if she had eaten well before taking the laudanum, traces of it will disappear faster. It is also very hard to detect laudanum in the stomach if it has been taken for some time over a regular period.'

'So, make haste,' Thomas summed up the doctor's thoughts.

'Yes. She's not long buried,' Dr Nevins said.

Harry added, 'We'll talk with her sons and see about an exhumation. But it seems as good a cause of death as any and will give them some peace.'

'It would make sense,' Thomas said. 'If she was hallucinating and thought she could fly, then leaping from the bridge was one way to launch into flight. But then we have the question of the source of the drug.'

'Exactly. Who is supplying the drug to Mr Rodgers in the first instance?' Dr Nevins asked.

'And how did Raymond Rodgers get his estranged wife to take the drug if she wasn't living at home?' Harry mused.

'One more question, about an older case, if I may?' Thomas asked.

'Go ahead. My patients are not the type who sit in the waiting room getting impatient and it is refreshing to discuss the case with the living for a change,' Dr Nevins joked.

'For a change? You've been discussing cases with the dead?' Thomas asked in jest.

'Regularly,' Dr Nevins said with a smile. 'They give me many insights without words, and I always get the last word in.'

'That's a relief,' Harry said. 'We thought you might have taken up soothsaying.'

The doctor laughed. 'In some cases that might have gleaned me more information. What is your question?' he asked Thomas.

'There's been several jumpers in the last month. Two ladies both jumping to their death from the Victoria Bridge, a gentleman who chose a steep slope at South Brisbane as the unfortunate site for his demise, and the recent death at the asylum,' Thomas said. 'I'm seeking a connection, if there is any. What do you recall of those cases?'

Dr Nevins nodded, aware of all four deaths. 'If there is nothing suspicious about a death, we do not do an autopsy, or if the doctor's death certificate advises a knowledge of a long-term illness that contributed to the victim's demise. In the case of the gentlemen at the cliffs, it was an accident. He was with a small party and lost his footing. There were witnesses and the family was most distressed.'

'I recall that one,' Harry said. 'Burton and his partner, Lou, investigated it,' he told Thomas. 'The family did their best to save his life but to no avail.'

Dr Nevins continued. 'The other female who fell to her death from the Victoria Bridge had been ill. Her doctor's certificate said she had been in chronic pain for some time. She chose to put herself out of it.'

Thomas sighed. 'Right, so unlikely that there was a link between those deaths.'

'Very unlikely,' Dr Nevins concurred. 'As for the recent death at the asylum, it is a regular occurrence – they are insane of course, and other than the drug on the deceased's breath which may have been used for medicinal reasons, I believe he took his own life.'

'The whole thing's crazy,' Thomas muttered.

'Always happy to take another look at the bodies if you are looking for something in particular, like narcotic poisons that can be tricky to detect,' Dr Nevins added.

They thanked Patrick and headed out of doors only to run into their police colleagues, Burton, and Lou.

'If it isn't the department's star pair,' Lou teased with a friendly nod to Thomas before encompassing Harry. 'How are you, gents?'

'Excellent. A fine morning to be visiting the dead,' Harry said, holding the door open for the men.

'Which body were you inspecting?' Burton asked, removing his hat and slicking down his hair. He was the same age as Thomas and they had trained together as young officers, but his career had not been as high flying.

'Raymond Rodgers,' Thomas said.

'Ah yes, husband of the jumper. Tough to prove anything with that one when he was miles from the scene.' Burton chuckled.

'And which corpse are you visiting?' Thomas asked.

'You heard about the fire last night at the Exhibition Building?' Lou asked.

Thomas and Harry looked surprised. 'Did someone die?' Harry asked.

'Indeed. We're not sure if they were in the wrong place at the wrong time, or if they caused the fire, or were conveniently disposed of in it, but we hope Patrick will know,' Burton said.

They bade each other farewell and Thomas and Harry continued on their route.

'We've given the boys a day to deal with their father's death,' Harry said, 'I suspected they didn't need an hour, but I'll be wanting to test their alibis.'

'They'll cover each other,' Thomas said. 'Who wouldn't?'

With some clearer direction of what they were looking for, the two men walked with more purpose as they set off to visit the boys at the bakery.

*****

There was a handful of customers in the bakery when the men arrived, and the smell of fresh bread had Thomas's mouth watering. He never ate enough on a case and he was always on a case. The store had not closed for the day to mourn the passing of the young men's father; they had not shed a tear. Thomas and Harry waited until the bakery was empty to address the boys.

'We've been expecting you,' Claude, the middle boy, said, his face masked with suspicion.

'We wanted to give you some mourning time but clearly you didn't need it,' Thomas said, indicating the shop was open for business and none of the boys appeared upset to him.

'There's plenty to keep us busy, and we've got rent to make,' Silas, the eldest, said.

'The only thing I'm mourning is that he didn't die years ago,' Claude said, not caring how his comments might be construed.

Thomas noted the look that passed between the two eldest boys – a glance from Silas to Claude no doubt warning him to watch what was said in front of himself and Harry.

'We've got some information about your father's death,' Harry said. 'Would you like to talk here before another customer enters or should we talk with you Silas, and you can relay the information?'

'We want to know, please,' Jesse, the youngest, spoke up.

'It won't take long,' Thomas said and told them of the drug and then he requested to exhume their mother. He noted both boys looked to Silas, who addressed them directly.

'The grave is only freshly dug, and the headstone has not yet gone on…' He looked embarrassed and turned to the two detectives. 'Our father would not give us the money to order a headstone for our mother, so we are saving for it.'

'You must be the sole benefactors of your father's will and I believe your father had insured your mother's life. You will receive that too, will you not?' Thomas asked.

'In good time,' Silas said. 'But we don't want to move back home. We're going to sell that and the first thing we'll do is honour our mother with a decent grave.'

'You are good lads,' Harry said, admiring them.

'I think it would be good to know if Mum was drugged. It will explain why she…' Silas's voice drifted off and he cleared his throat. 'I think it will be fine to exhume Mum. Claude? Jesse?' The brothers agreed to the request with a curt nod, and Thomas thanked them.

'Do you know if your father had a history of using that drug or have you ever seen him administer it?' Harry asked.

They shook their heads in the negative.

'Our father was against anything medicinal. He believed God provided all we needed, including our fate, which shouldn't be fought with drugs,' Claude said and rolled his eyes.

Harry smiled. 'So, he held that view alone?'

'Absolutely,' Silas said. 'Why would you not take advantage of the progression of medicine or of anything, for that matter? We're always looking at new baking practices.'

And then Thomas asked the question he had to ask: 'Can you tell me where you all were at the time of your father's death… mid-afternoon, Wednesday?'

'We were all here,' Silas said, 'the shop does not close until 4pm. If we stay open that bit later, we make extra from the schoolchildren coming in for treats and those wanting bargains on bread that did not sell this morning. Not everyone can afford to pay full price.'

Thomas couldn't help but be impressed by the young men. 'We'll be in touch as soon as we have some results and rest assured, we will return your mother's body to her resting place and leave it in the respectable fashion in which we found it.'

'Thank you, Detective,' Silas said.

As the men got further afield, Thomas asked his partner, 'What do you think?'

'I think if they killed their father, I want them to get away with it,' Harry answered honestly.

'Couldn't agree more,' Thomas said. 'We can rule out the cousin, Mrs Flora Bignell. I doubt she would have the strength to cause the injury Mr Rodgers was sporting.'

'I suspect you are right. Let's go and organise the digging up of Mrs Rodgers then. The sooner we have those results, the better.'

Chapter 16

The asylum came into view – large and looming, full of misery and hope, pain and redemption. Moments later, Matilda and Georgina alighted from the hansom and entered through the gates.

'It is so foreboding, isn't it?' Matilda said. 'I can't imagine the fear of being brought here as a patient, wondering if you would ever escape and scared of how you might be treated. Especially if you were sane like poor Mrs Rodgers.'

'Terrifying,' Georgina agreed. 'I would storm the fort demanding to be released, which would probably make me look more insane! But unlike Hilda Rodgers, my father would never make me marry a man that I did not love or who was unkind, thank goodness.'

'Nor mine. We are lucky,' Matilda agreed, giving a silent prayer of thanks for the family she was blessed with, although as a girl she might have happily traded a couple of annoying big brothers for a sister.

Georgina took in a deep breath as they walked up the path. 'Foreboding aside, it is so lovely to get out of the office.

I love my work and all the ladies at the *Women's Journal*, but I miss being outdoors as much as I used to be.'

Matilda turned to her. 'How so?'

'My parents are farmers, out Toowoomba way,' she explained. 'I was outside more than I was inside. Riding, helping with the animals. Some days I wonder if I should just go home.'

'And what of your work? Would you just draw for pleasure?' Matilda asked.

'Perhaps. Or create works for pleasure or sale or take commissions for portraits. I haven't given it a great deal of thought as yet, but confess I am a little homesick for the space and the light of the morning, the green of the fields,' she said and sighed.

'I am sure the sight of the confines of an asylum does not help,' Matilda offered sympathetically, and no sooner had she said the words, than the ladies heard a piercing scream and voices shouting. Several men in white uniforms ran from the front of the building and around to the side, where a small crowd of patients and staff were gathering. Several patients pointed upwards and were agitated.

'Oh, my goodness, let's go and see,' Matilda said, and Georgina needed no encouragement. The ladies lifted their skirts slightly and hurried up the path as fast as they could without losing their hats. The latest fashions with the slimmer long skirts and blouses allowed for a little more speed than the layers of yesteryear.

'Are we to expect drama every time we visit?' Georgina asked. 'I am not sure I can handle the excitement.'

Elijah, in his dark suit and the matron in uniform, ran out of the front of the building and headed towards the gathered crowd.

'There's your brother. It must be one of the ladies, his patient maybe,' Georgina said, rushing along beside Matilda.

Matilda's gaze connected with Elijah's, and he stopped momentarily as the matron rushed on. His dark eyes wide with alarm, he raised his hand to stop them as they neared.

'Matilda, Miss Urry, please stop there. You may be exposed to a traumatic sight otherwise,' he ordered and ran on.

They looked at each other and then continued to walk quickly to the scene of the action, following some distance behind Elijah.

'We may be able to help,' Matilda said, justifying their actions, and Georgina nodded.

As they rounded the corner, they came across a small group and looked up to where everyone was staring. At the top of the building, at least three levels up, Meredith – the tall, graceful dressmaker – stood in the frame of a window, nothing preventing her from falling to her death below.

'No, not dear Meredith,' Matilda gasped.

'But why?' Georgina asked and then added, 'Oh, I guess she is in an insane asylum.'

'Stay back everyone,' Dr O'Shea said, with eminent authority as he stood in front of the swelling crowd. Elijah and the matron joined him. Another man who appeared to be a doctor – the very same man Matilda had seen but not spoken with the last visit – arrived beside Elijah.

'Get the patients back to their rooms,' Dr O'Shea ordered the staff who were not having an easy job of it.

'Dr O'Shea, I'm ready,' Meredith called from the floors above.

Matilda moved closer now, nearby Elijah, who had not noticed them yet. Matilda heard him ask, 'How did she get the bars off that window? I checked just recently that there were no opportunities to fall from great heights.' He was looking across the span of the building where bars were firmly affixed on every other window.

Meredith stepped out a little further and Elijah stepped forward. 'Meredith, not yet. I need to check your wings,' he said.

Matilda saw the matron gave Elijah a bemused look and then she glanced at Dr O'Shea.

'Remember, you said your wings were hurting last time I checked?' Elijah continued trying to buy time while the orderlies made their way to Meredith's level to pull her back.

'But I'm ready, Dr Hayward, I am sure of it.'

'You haven't got your flying certificate, have you?' he asked, and she stopped and looked confused.

Matilda grasped Georgina's hand as Meredith lost her footing and the crowd below shrieked with panic. Meredith steadied herself.

Elijah continued. 'Your certificate. You need it to fly. It's white and gold, and we can get it framed. You better get that first, Meredith, it's very important.'

'My certificate,' she said, thinking about it. 'Do you have it?'

'Yes, it has just arrived. It is in my office. I need to give it to you before you fly or you won't be ready – you've earned it, Meredith, we must make it official.'

Matilda held her breath as she and everyone present watched Meredith thinking through Elijah's words. Meredith then gave a small smile of pleasure, as if she had indeed earned that certificate.

And then arms grabbed and snatched her from behind and pulled her back into the room. The windows were firmly shut, and an audible sigh of relief was heard from staff, while the patients murmured with excitement. Elijah exhaled; his relief palpable.

'Well done, Dr Hayward, very quick thinking,' Dr O'Shea said, tapping Elijah on the back.

Elijah thanked him, but Matilda knew her brother as well as she knew herself. She recognised his expression, his jaw locked with frustration. Beside him, Matilda saw the other, shorter doctor, shake his head slightly.

'Criminal,' he muttered, and Elijah snapped to look at him. The doctor turned and left as abruptly as he arrived, joining the dispersing group. Some patients cried; others clapped with excitement. Matron hurried them along.

'You were brilliant, Elijah,' Matilda said, relief rushing through her, and he turned and appeared surprised to find his sister and Miss Urry right behind him. He had been so focused.

'Not really,' Elijah said modestly. 'Meredith told me of her plans to fly last time we spoke and that she was growing wings.' He turned to Georgina. 'Miss Urry,' he said, greeting her formerly now, with a small bow.

He started to walk back to the main building with the ladies and Dr O'Shea. Elijah made the introductions: 'Dr O'Shea, may I introduce my sister, Miss Matilda Hayward, and the *Women's Journal* illustrator, Miss Georgina Urry? They are volunteering.'

'We are old friends,' Georgina said, and Dr O'Shea looked pleased on seeing her.

'Indeed we are, lovely to see you again, Georgina, and delightful to meet you, Miss Hayward,' Dr O'Shea said, addressing each lady in turn.

'Quite a job you have, Dr O'Shea,' Matilda said, looking up at the tall man in front of her.

'Not for the faint-hearted,' he agreed, returning her smile. Matilda imagined he would be very good at his job; he was charming and drew in the recipient of his gaze with his large smile and warm nature.

Turning he said, 'You have a beautiful sister, Dr Hayward, and it is a delightful surprise to run into you again, Georgina, and here of all places.' The four ascended the stairs to the reception.

'May I ask where you have met previously?' Elijah enquired as he and Matilda eyed the pair with curiosity.

'Yes, indeed,' Dr O'Shea responded. 'I was resident at the General Hospital in Toowoomba for several years before taking this post, and I occasionally did a country run. I had the pleasure of getting to know Georgina and her family very well,' he said.

'You're a country girl, then?' Elijah asked, taking in Miss Urry's appearance, which Matilda noticed and looked at from her brother's perspective. There was something unique about Georgina – a confidence and assurance that possibly came from being a country girl and not fussed by city formalities and expectations. Maybe it came from a love of the land and no pressure to marry or partner well. Whatever it was, she was a unique and handsome woman, if not somewhat unpolished and colt-like in appearance.

'Country girl through and through,' Georgina agreed. 'My parents own a farm in the Darling Downs.'

'You are being modest, my dear,' Dr O'Shea laughed. 'William and Jane Urry own one of the state's biggest cattle stations. You'd do well to secure the hand of Miss Urry,' Dr O'Shea said with a wink and a laugh in Elijah's direction, which Matilda noticed made Elijah redden. He wasn't one for being the centre of attention or framed for marriage, but most gentlemen were not keen on that concept, she imagined.

'I am sure, Mr Urry would prefer his daughter won the heart of a veterinarian than a doctor,' Elijah suggested, and Georgina laughed.

'There's truth in that,' she agreed. 'There are many trying times on the farm, and a skilled veterinarian would not go unwelcomed. But I suspect Father would prefer my choice was one of love, not concern for the cattle,' she said with a smile Elijah's way.

They stopped at the entrance before going their separate ways.

'Please give my best to your parents, Georgina. How are William and Jane?'

'Much the same, but they'll be delighted to know I have seen you,' Georgina said. 'Dad is still working long hours and preferring the company of cows to people, and Mum is hellbent on organising everything from dinner to the local country women's annual charity dance.'

Dr O'Shea laughed at her description. 'All is well then,' he agreed and including Matilda, he added, 'I look forward to seeing you both here brightening our work abode.' He gave the ladies a departing nod.

Matilda turned to Elijah. 'Are you all right, Elijah?'

'Thank you, yes. Disaster averted for now. But I must go and tend to Meredith and find out what drove her to attempt to jump. Plus, find out why the restraints were not on that window. I shall see you both during my rounds,' Elijah said.

'I hope so,' Georgina said, and Matilda gave a small laugh and Elijah grinned before turning away.

With Elijah gone, the ladies looped arms and continued through to the volunteer rooms.

'I am too forward, aren't I?' Georgina said with a laugh. 'My mother finds me quite mortifying at times.'

'I think you are refreshing and just perfect as you are,' Matilda said and squeezed her new friend's hand. 'Come, let us see what madness can top today's performance!'

Chapter 17

Elijah thanked the matron and orderlies that he passed for their assistance as he made his way down the sterile hallway of the asylum, his footfalls echoing around the walls. The older wing where patients were kept in solitary rooms was cold and hostile. He was sure it did nothing to aid in their recovery. Elijah wanted to check on Meredith and to try to understand why today, of all days, she determined she needed to fly. Then, he intended to find out why the bars were not on the sewing room window. He stopped an orderly whom he recognised from the hospital wards.

'Where have they taken Mrs Meredith Martineau?' Elijah asked.

'The jumper?' he said with an amused look which Elijah did not return.

'If that were your mother or sister or aunt, would you find the situation as amusing?' Elijah asked.

'No, no Doctor, sorry.' The orderly cleared his throat and sobered. 'She's been restrained in one of the padded cells, Doctor. The last one on your left,' he said and quickly resumed his journey.

Elijah moved to the last room and glanced in through the small window available. He watched the tall but frail woman rocking on the bed's edge, her body enclosed in a white straitjacket; the long sleeves tied together to confine her arms from movement. Unnecessary, Elijah thought, angry at the orderlies' use of the restraint. Meredith had no intention of harming anyone except herself. He opened the door, and her gaze flew up to him.

'Dr Hayward, do you have my certificate?' she asked, her eyes lit up with anticipation.

'It's being gold stamped as we speak,' he said and knelt nearby to study her.

'Let us remove this troublesome jacket, shall we?' he said and began to unclip the jacket to free her. She allowed Elijah to turn her to remove the offending garment. Underneath, she wore the thin grey work dress that many of the women prisoners wore.

As she turned to face him, the smell of a narcotic on her breath hit Elijah.

'What have you taken today, Meredith, do you remember?'

'I had my toast and tea for breakfast, but I did not partake in morning tea. I didn't want to feel heavy before I was to fly,' she said most sincerely.

'Of course,' Elijah said, rising and placing the straitjacket near the door to take with him on departure. He returned and sat beside Meredith.

'Did you take any special medicine to help with your wings?'

'Just the potion I am meant to take.'

'Right. Who gave you the special potion?' Elijah pushed.

'It was with my breakfast, or was it before then that I had it?' She thought for a moment, then began to rock again.

'Meredith, have you had this potion before?' Elijah asked.

'Several times to help grow my wings and then you are supposed to take it on the day you intend to fly, like today,' she said with a hint of surprise in her voice, as if Elijah, being a doctor, should know this.

'Right, yes, I remember now. Who suggested you should have this special potion?'

'The angels, of course. They can fly already,' Meredith said.

Elijah refrained from sighing. Perhaps she might be more lucid in a few hours, he thought.

'When was the window opened for your flight?' he tried again.

'Always,' she said.

Elijah gave up. 'Meredith, I would like you to lie down and rest for a while now. There will be no flying today… the weather is turning bad.'

'Ah, best then,' she agreed.

He helped her to lie down and covered her with a blanket.

'I'll come back and see how you are later. But save your strength for now.'

'I shall, thank you, Dr Hayward.'

'You can come to me anytime, Meredith,' he said and watched her for a moment. She was almost asleep before he left the cell, the drug wearing off. Elijah knew that smell and now he intended to go to her bed and the sewing room and investigate. This was not a result of Meredith's madness. This was inflicted. Someone gave her a drug. But why? Who would want to bring about the death of such a harmless woman? Elijah had no answers.

Somewhere, somehow, someone has administered Meredith a reasonable sized dose of laudanum. Enough to make her euphoric. Enough to make her think – with the right encouragement – that she could fly.

Chapter 18

Thomas paced the length of his office. He had been pacing for only a short time before Harry appeared, hat and coat in hand, in his doorway.

'All done,' Harry said. 'They will exhume Mrs Hilda Rodgers' body late today and take it straight to the morgue. Ah, you are doing the pacing thing.' Harry observed. 'Best we go through everything from the top then.' He entered and placed his coat and hat down over the chair opposite Thomas's desk.

'It would help,' Thomas agreed gratefully.

They both turned, hearing a loud knock to find their colleagues and partners, Burton and Lou, entering.

'Gentlemen,' Burton said, 'surprised to find you here and not out there solving crime,' he added, waving his hand in the general direction of the streets.

'All our cases are up to date,' Harry said, and Lou's mouth fell open with surprise.

'No, really?' Burton said and then grinned. 'You almost had me going then.'

Thomas chuckled. 'To what do we owe the honour of this visit?'

'An honour indeed,' Burton agreed. He took a seat, though uninvited and brushed a hand over his dark and rough appearance. 'A bit of news that might interest you.' He nodded to his partner, Lou, who took it upon himself to explain.

'The body we pulled from the Brisbane Exhibition Building fire was a middle-aged man by the name of Finch Turner, of no occupation and no fixed address. He had been sleeping rough for a few weeks; his wife threw him out,' Lou stated.

'Poor fellow,' Harry said. He was the most soft-hearted among the pack.

'Yeah, well thanks for that,' Thomas said, 'but we're not collecting cases this week. You can keep that one.'

Burton gave him a wry look and nudged Lou to continue.

'His previous place of abode was the men's asylum at Wacol,' Lou added.

Both Thomas and Harry's eyes widened with interest.

'Reel them in, Lou,' Burton said, and Lou grinned.

'The coroner thinks he might have taken a fall before being swallowed by the fire. A fall from a great height.'

'And, he had a nice life insurance policy, which the wife will benefit from, not that she's a suspect at this stage,' Burton added.

'Lads, you can come by anytime,' Harry said gratefully.

'Where is his body now? Still with the coroner?' Thomas asked.

Burton stood and stuck his hat back on his head. 'It is. Patrick said he'd hang on to Mr Turner until you ventured over to see him. Thought you'd be excited by that find.'

'Another one,' Thomas muttered. Frowning, he paced again while he thought, as if no one else was in the room. Harry thanked the boys as they departed with an amused look in Thomas's direction.

'I want to get every recent patient release and death record from that asylum,' Thomas said, looking over at Harry.

'We can do that, but first, let's do it the old-fashioned way. Let's go over what we've got,' Harry said, attempting to centre his charge.

'You're right, yes,' Thomas said and exhaled.

Harry grabbed the chalk and offered to write. 'We want to be able to read it later.'

Thomas grimaced and lowered himself onto the edge of his desk. 'We have too many loose ends and no obvious connections. I am not sure what is a crime and what is not among the lot,' Thomas said and sighed.

'You do have it bad,' Harry teased. He began to write on the board. 'Not including the two earlier jumpers that the coroner ruled out as accidental and ill, we now have three deaths by falling and one by beating; we know that one to be murder.' He wrote on the board the names Raymond Rodgers, Hilda Rodgers, Percy Sturgess, and Finch Turner.

'All four have a connection to the asylum,' Thomas said as Harry drew an asylum image and connected it to all of them. 'Not bad,' Thomas rated the drawing.

'I'm a man of many talents. You should see my bird

drawings,' Harry joked. 'So, of our four victims, one was a current asylum patient, two were ex-patients and died since leaving the asylum,' Harry continued.

'Suspects…' Thomas began. 'Raymond Rodgers benefited financially from his wife's death, and the three Rodgers boys benefited from their mother's and father's deaths. Our recent asylum jumper, Percy Sturgess, had nothing in the world to leave to anyone apparently – but maybe his wife on the outside wants to remarry. There's a motive. Our fire victim, Finch Turner's wife will be rewarded financially from her husband's death.'

'A bottle of laudanum was found at the scene,' Harry continued, writing it up, 'but none of the drug in Raymond Rodger's system. We're yet to find out if there's any in Hilda Rodgers and Finch Turner's systems – if the fire has not burned away the evidence in Mr Turner's body. We know it was on Percy Sturgess' breath after the asylum fall.'

'And if there is none in Hilda Rodgers' system, then did Raymond Rodgers's killer own the bottle and lose it during his attack?' Thomas rose from sitting on the edge of his desk. 'Too many loose ends. My gut tells me that there's some connection to the asylum, but I can't see any benefit for the asylum in these deaths, except more empty beds.' He shook his head in frustration.

'Best not to storm there demanding their files until we get those results… it could all be a coincidence,' Harry said.

'That's exactly why I want to see the files of every asylum-related death in the last six months, in residence and discharged,' Thomas said restlessly. 'But first, let's hurry the

coroner up. Patrick has two bodies now to test for drugs
– Hilda Rodgers and Finch Turner. Let's hope he moves it
along before someone else falls from a great height.'

*****

Elijah heard footsteps hurrying behind him and turned to
find Dr O'Shea rushing down the hallway. He stopped and
waited.

'Dr Hayward, excellent, just the man I was looking for,'
Dr O'Shea said, catching his breath.

'Is everything all right?' Elijah asked, concerned.

'Yes, yes, nothing to worry about. I am just behind today
and trying to catch up.'

'Well, you have found me,' Elijah said. 'I have just checked
on Meredith and am doing the rounds to check that the
patients and staff are not too distressed from Meredith's
attempt at flight.'

'Yes, good thinking. I shall join you. I like to reach out
and meet everyone regularly,' he said, and smoothed down
his vest and jacket after his brief run.

'Of course,' Elijah welcomed him but found it most odd,
especially if he was as busy as he said. At the hospital where
Elijah worked before, the manager would not have had the
time to be social, but Dr O'Shea was a charismatic man.

They entered the volunteers' room and several of the
volunteer ladies and patients looked up and greeted them,
including Matilda and Georgina, who sat nearby with their
charges.

'Hello ladies,' Dr O'Shea said. 'Lovely to see you all being so active.'

Winifred, the Asylum Volunteer Manager rose to greet them. She wore a large badge bearing only her first name, but informality was insisted on in the volunteer area. She moved closer to the two gentlemen to assist if needed.

'Dr O'Shea and Dr Hayward, welcome, what a lovely surprise.'

Dr O'Shea smiled and thanked her. 'I try to visit as much as I can. I like to see what masterpieces you have all created,' he said, looking around and including everyone with his smile.

Elijah gave a small smile and bow. The effusiveness was not something he could convey, but he was every bit as genuine in his care and attention.

Winifred turned to Elijah. 'Well done this morning, Dr Hayward, that was traumatic,' she said, with an exaggerated sigh and her hand placed on her heart.

'It was indeed, Winifred. Thank goodness it had a happy ending,' Elijah agreed. He lowered his voice. 'I've just seen Meredith. She is sleeping now but won't come back here or to the dressmaking studio today. Were any of the patients overly distressed?'

Winifred lowered her voice. 'Birdie was initially, but I don't think it was out of concern for Meredith. More likely, she wanted to be part of the adventure, dare I say. The rest of the ladies quickly settled in once they became occupied.'

'Good. I firmly believe in keeping busy,' Elijah said.

'As do I,' Dr O'Shea said, re-joining their conversation and backing up Elijah.

The tall, red-haired volunteer manager touched her hair several times as she spoke with Elijah; he often had that effect on women… his tall, dark, handsome and quiet demeanour pulling them in. But Dr O'Shea was not to be outdone, he liked to be the centre of attention, and, unlike Elijah, who let the matter lie and felt no need to revisit it, Dr O'Shea jumped in feet first.

'Now ladies, I assure you that Meredith is fine and there is nothing to be concerned about!' he exclaimed. 'Is everyone happy?'

There were smiles all around and several calls of "Yes" in response to his question.

'Excellent,' he said, beaming. 'Miss Hayward, Miss Urry, have you had a tour of our fine establishment yet?' Dr O'Shea singled them out as new volunteers but did not wait for their response. 'Perhaps you should join Dr Hayward and me as we do the afternoon rounds.'

Elijah smiled, pleased with the suggestion. He wanted to study Meredith's room and the dressmaking studio but had no excuse to linger. Now he could do so for longer if the ladies distracted Dr O'Shea. He also had no objection to spending a little more time in the company of the fascinating Miss Urry.

'Excellent idea,' Winifred said and clapped her hands. 'Your charges can work on with their projects in your absence.'

As Matilda and Georgina happily accepted and rose to take part, Winifred addressed Elijah: 'I don't suppose that Dr O'Shea had told you about the tours?'

'No. Tours?' Elijah asked with dread, assuming he would need to take medical inspectors through the building.

'Once a month he provides our new volunteers – male and female – with a tour of the facilities,' she explained.

'Oh, good. Why?' he asked, confused. Elijah smiled at Matilda as she joined him.

'Often we get called upon to assist in different areas – with showering, calming patients, moving patients, or as needed. So, we like the volunteers to have a look around and then advise us where they might be prepared to help, other than just in the arts and craft area.'

'I see,' Elijah said, not liking the risk nor his sister being exposed to it.

'Dr O'Shea likes to do it himself, so he can determine if the volunteers have the capability to assist. It is one thing to want and another thing to do,' she said, raising an eyebrow as though vast years of experience had proved that to her.

Elijah bit his tongue from saying it was just an opportunity for Dr O'Shea to grandstand again, as seemed to be his wont; he struggled to understand that type of personality. Elijah thanked Winifred, whose confidence he appreciated, and with Matilda in tow, followed Dr O'Shea and Miss Urry to the next part of the asylum. His rational mind analysed why Dr O'Shea's need for attention bothered him. He had always been content to be the quiet one among the more exuberant members of his family – not seeking the spotlight. Why should Dr O'Shea's personality alienate him so?

Then he realised why. He did not like the way Dr O'Shea charmed and engaged Miss Georgina Urry. And, he did not know if Dr O'Shea was married, but clearly, he found Miss Urry splendid company – they shared a joke again and laughed between them as they walked on ahead. Then and there he decided he'd best act soon if he intended to court Miss Urry.

Chapter 19

Matilda felt a mixture of excitement and dread. She was keen to tour the asylum facility and, as Mrs Lawson had suggested, expand her life experience, but she was also a little fearful of what she might see within the confines of the asylum walls. A terrible feeling stirred within her – that but for the grace of God, it could be herself locked away in one of these rooms, at the mercy of the staff and living among the stark and sterile conditions.

'We don't have any ghosts, well none that I've encountered,' Dr O'Shea said as he led the way. He raised his voice for Matilda's benefit as she walked slightly behind, aside Elijah.

'Well, what ghost in their right mind would stay here once their soul had left?' Georgina asked. 'I can think of ten places I'd rather haunt.'

Dr O'Shea chuckled. 'A valid point, Georgina.'

Matilda looked to Elijah, who was smiling and watching Georgina. When he turned to face her, Matilda raised an enquiring eyebrow.

He grimaced at her, and they continued.

'We are passing through the wards now where the female patients sleep. You will see we are quite overcrowded, but there is nothing to be done for it,' Dr O'Shea said, looking from one end of the room to the other. 'Lord knows I am constantly trying to secure additional funding for expansion.'

Matilda's eyes widened at the size of the room and the number of beds in it, all packed closely together, all the same, and with little in terms of warmth or comfort.

'Is every one of these beds taken?' Matilda asked.

'Every single one,' Elijah responded.

'Goodness,' Matilda said, thinking of her own large, private and beautifully decorated room at home.

Georgina asked Dr O'Shea a question, and they continued through the room as he answered.

Matilda moved closer to Elijah. 'Are you trying to find out more about Meredith and why she wanted to jump?' she asked hurriedly.

'Yes, I am her doctor now and I certainly did not administer her anything that would have brought on that psychosis. But I can't play the detective,' he said, his voice laced with frustration. 'I've only been here a week and my queries must look to be medically related.'

Matilda nodded and raised her voice.

'So where do my ladies sleep – Birdie, Meredith and Esther, assuming they have the same bunk every night?'

'Indeed,' Elijah answered. 'Routine is important. I believe your ladies are dispersed in here, but I do know that is Meredith's bed there by the corner.'

'I shall leave her a small ribbon under her pillow if I may?' Matilda said, 'a little gift after her harrowing morning.'

'That's very thoughtful,' Elijah said, smiling at her, his eyes conveying his thanks.

They walked to Meredith's bed together and while Matilda blocked the view of Dr O'Shea as best she could, Elijah patted down the bed, looked under it, and quickly lifted the pillow. He gave her a small nod to indicate he had finished, and they turned to catch up. Dr O'Shea was looking through the large windows to the gardens below and a group of patients hard at work.

'We call this moral therapy,' he said, watching the women actively involved in garden duties. He pushed open the window enough to call down on them. 'Looking wonderful ladies, keep up the good work.'

Several of the patients looked up and returned his smile, another looked stricken that someone from heaven was calling down to her and fell on her knees. Dr O'Shea ignored this and turned back to his guests as Elijah frowned with concern until he saw a nurse coming to tend to her.

'Let's look at the work rooms next; that's where our occupational therapy is put into practice,' Dr O'Shea marched on.

'I'd love to see the sewing room,' Matilda said. 'I think it is amazing that you produce so much of what you need on the premises – all the uniforms and patients' outfits, I hear?'

Dr O'Shea smiled with pride. 'Yes, I started a lot of those activities. It is good for patients to work, and ideal if they contribute something useful, if they can. Wouldn't you say, Dr Hayward?'

'I am in complete agreement, Dr O'Shea,' Elijah responded. 'There's a lot to be said for the dignity of usefulness.'

'I don't know what I would do if you took me in as a patient,' Georgina said, looking concerned. 'Other than illustrate, I would be quite useless unless you brought me a cow and I could milk her.'

Dr O'Shea laughed and greeted patients and staff as he went along the corridors.

'Hmm, a care farm and animal husbandry, I like that idea,' Dr O'Shea said, seriously considering it.

'I suspect you have many talents, Miss Urry,' Elijah said at her side, 'and your illustrating skills for one, are proving to brighten the lives of our volunteers.'

Georgina blushed, which Matilda noticed and thought most unusual for the unflappable country girl. Then Georgina's eyes widened, and Matilda followed her gaze into a room with padded walls, a bed with straps and some odd devices at the end. It looked like a medical torture chamber. Further along, was a large room with half a dozen bath tubs covered in rubber mats and room only for a head to push through. Matilda shuddered at the thought.

Dr O'Shea stopped in the hallway and pointed out two rooms. 'The one on the left is the library which patients are welcomed and encouraged to use, and on the right is the dressmaking and mending room.'

'Ooh, do let's have a look at the library,' Georgina said, engaging Dr O'Shea and pulling him into the room. She gave Matilda a quick nod.

'She's onto us,' Matilda said to Elijah, 'such a clever girl.

'Come.' They quickly entered the dressmaking room and Matilda greeted a couple of ladies who sat darning. Elijah went to the windows and studied the bars. They were all intact and secured now but there were fresh scratches on the bars that had been removed.

'Hello, what beautiful stitching,' Matilda said, admiring one lady's work. 'Where does your friend, Meredith, sit when she works?'

'That's her table in the corner. But you'd better not sit there. She gets cranky,' the patient answered.

Another lady beside her nodded in agreement and looked at the desk fearfully.

Matilda nodded towards the sewing machine and desk in the corner and Elijah quickly checked the area. 'Thank you, in that case I'll take your advice and definitely not sit there.'

'I am out of white thread!' a patient exclaimed loudly in front of Matilda, holding up her needle as if proof was required. 'Meredith gets it for me,' she said, looking around as if Meredith would suddenly materialise.

'Allow me to fetch some,' Matilda said, and Elijah moved out of her way and just in time as Dr O'Shea and Georgina entered.

'Just getting some thread,' Matilda told them in a sing-song voice. She opened a couple of drawers in the desk and then saw a small sewing basket. Opening it, she proclaimed, 'Here is it then, white thread.' She grabbed the thread and her eyes widened at the small medicine bottle in the basket's corner. Matilda grabbed a handkerchief-sized piece of fabric from the bottom of the basket, wrapped the bottle in it and, turning, slipped it into the pocket of her skirt while holding the thread high in her other hand. 'Sew on my dear,' she said, giving it to the lady in question. 'You are doing beautiful work.'

'Onward then?' Dr O'Shea asked, and they all agreed.

Matilda glanced at Elijah and patted her pocket. His eyes widened and moving closer, she slipped him the bottle. They had all they needed… for now.

Chapter 20

The matron looked at Thomas as if his request was preposterous. She rose from her seat at the Asylum for the Insane reception desk in the general admission building and leaned forward to address him.

'Am I to understand, that you want the file of every patient who died in the last six months and every patient released in that time frame?' she asked.

'Precisely, Madam,' Thomas said.

'Detectives, you are aware this is an asylum, are you not?' she said, looking from Thomas to Harry with a supercilious attitude and a wave of her hand to the surrounding walls.

'Indeed, I am acutely aware of that,' Thomas said with a curt nod.

'Death is a regular occurrence,' she continued, 'and we have never been questioned before about our death register.'

'How long will it take to gather the files?' Thomas asked, cutting to the chase and the business at hand.

The matron stood even straighter, no mean feat with her stout frame. Harry did his best not to smile. He enjoyed watching his young protégé come up against resistance.

'How long, indeed! I have an enormous workload so it will go on my list, and I'll get to it when humanly possible. That's the best I can do.'

Harry stepped in. 'We understand, but of course you would not want to obstruct an ongoing investigation. No civil servant would want that on their record.'

'I am quite fervent in my duty to the community,' she said proudly, then added, 'what sort of investigation?'

Harry ignored the question. 'How many deaths would you estimate in those six months, Matron?' he asked, curious to know exactly how large the workload would be to pull the files.

The matron was torn between wanting to look knowledgeable and wanting to move the troublesome detectives away from her desk as soon as possible. She thought for a moment, pursing her lips and then answered: 'Approximately fifteen to twenty per month, so in a six-month period, one might expect ninety deaths or more, Detective.'

'Truly? That many?' Thomas exclaimed.

'We have many aged and destitute that we take in as well, Detectives. Abandoned by their families and with no money to feed themselves or means of housing, they are at the end of their journey so their deaths are expected.'

Thomas nodded. 'Noted. Thank you, Matron, we'll call back then in, say, a week? Is that enough time to gather ninety files?'

'I cannot guarantee that, Detective, but I'll do my best.' She added, 'I would not want to stand in the way of the police force administering their duties.'

Thomas gave her a nod of thanks. 'We would like to speak with Dr Stephen O'Shea now, if we may?'

'You will find him in the men's ward, conducting family interviews,' she said and indicated the exit. 'I doubt he will see you this afternoon. You may need an appointment.'

'Family interviews?' Harry asked.

'After a patient is admitted, and if they have any family members who care, Dr O'Shea will meet with the family at the end of the patient's first month of admission to discuss progress. He will review his notes and those of either Dr McQuade or Dr Hayward, depending on whether it is a male or female patient,' the matron said in a rote voice that indicated this should be self-explanatory.

'We'll try our luck, thank you,' Thomas said.

She gave the detective a look that was hard to read – perhaps exasperation and impatience – but he could imagine she was pleased to be rid of him. 'Out this door and across the path, level two at the end of the hallway near the stairs.'

The gentleman thanked her and proceeded to the male wards.

'I hate obstinance,' Thomas muttered under his breath.

'I know,' Harry said and smiled at him. 'Brace yourself for some sights, then. Poor fellows.' He entered the men's ward as Thomas held open the door and they proceeded to the second level.

*****

Matilda stood by the window in the volunteers' room, looking out at the garden. It was a beautiful day, and the garden was a charming sight. For a moment, she forgot she was in an insane asylum. Nearby, Georgina illustrated several of the patients while her charges did their own drawings. Matilda had finished a round of poetry and writing exercises for fun and was just about to read to several of the ladies as they rested in the warmth of the sunbeams coming through the windows.

'It is time for my walk. I want to go to the garden,' a voice said beside her, and Matilda turned to see Kirra, a pretty, young aboriginal woman, quiet and gentle, tugging on her sleeve. Matilda was not sure why she was in the asylum, but many patients seemed to live on the edge of sanity.

'I, too, would like a stroll in the garden,' Matilda said, smiling at Kirra. 'I shall check with Winifred if we may.'

Kirra followed closely beside Matilda as they approached Winifred, the manager, for permission.

'Absolutely. What a fine idea,' Winifred said. 'Hannah might like some time in the garden too, she often does at this time of the day.'

Hearing her name, Hannah looked up and nodded. She rose, leaving her stitching on her chair and looped her arm through Matilda's. The three ladies proceeded to the garden.

'I know the best spot,' Kirra said, breaking away to lead them. 'Near the fountain.'

'Then we shall proceed there,' Matilda agreed, allowing herself to be held by Hannah who still gripped her arm. Matilda felt a wave of sadness for the two ladies, but contentment to bring some small degree of happiness into their day, even if it was just escorting them to the garden on this fine winter's afternoon.

The three ladies of different ages, backgrounds and histories proceeded to the large magnolia tree and the surrounding greenery. A hedge formed a small maze and the fountain in the middle created a tranquil setting.

Matilda inhaled the scent of the freshly cut grass and looked skyward to feel the warm winter sun on her face. She watched in comfortable silence as Hannah lowered herself to sit on the grass and proceeded to pull small weeds from the garden bed. Kirra dipped her hand in the fountain water and then pressed her fingers on the warm pavers.

'Kangaroo,' she said, creating an animal footprint that soon faded.

Matilda watched with delight. 'That is so clever, Kirra,' she offered, and the young woman looked over at her and smiled with pleasure. She pointed to something above Matilda's head and said 'lorikeet' as the bird flew by. Kirra returned to her animal footprints announcing 'duck' as her next creation.

Matilda moved closer to the maze, running her hand along its carefully manicured shape, unaware that danger was on the other side.

Chapter 21

The two detectives arrived at the offices on the second floor of the men's wing and found the interview office door closed. A sign on the door read '*Occupied*'. As Thomas raised his hand to knock, a nurse hurried along the corridor towards him.

'Hello, can I help you? Dr O'Shea is in a meeting, he will be another thirty minutes, possibly. Are you family?' she asked.

Thomas greeted the nurse and turned, leaving Harry to respond. He looked from the windows of the second floor to the grounds below. It startled him on seeing Matilda in the gardens with two patients. She was alone with them. Surely that cannot be normal, he thought. Even if they are harmless, there must be a risk associated with them, or they would not be patients in the first instance.

He frowned and shuffled uncomfortably, watching for her safety, admiring her in all her beauty among the garden. At least the other two ladies were in sitting position and Matilda standing if she needed to move quickly.

Then his heart lurched. Behind the hedge maze was a group of six male patients, all gardening with an orderly nearby. The orderly's attention waned as he glanced around, yawned, and occasionally commented on the gardening work being done.

One man wandered away. A big man in build, he wandered towards the maze… on the other side was Matilda, with the two ladies. Thomas returned his attention to the orderly, who had not realised one of his charges was missing.

Thomas attempted to push open the window, to call out.

'What is it?' Harry moved to join him and looked below. 'Ah, the lovely Miss Hayward.' Then he, too, saw the man approaching.

The patient was coming around the hedge now – a powerful man, unstable and full of delusions – he approached the three women. Approached Matilda.

Thomas banged against the window, trying to get the orderly's attention.

'Run, Thom,' Harry said, and Thomas needed no further encouragement. He took the stairs with the speed of lightning.

*****

Matilda stopped at the end of the hedge and turned to walk back to the ladies. She sensed a presence. Heard a groan. She wheeled around in fright. A large man, a patient in uniform, moved towards her. He leered.

Matilda cleared her throat. 'Hel–hello there,' she said,

frightened, stepping backwards. She glanced behind him. No one followed. No orderly. No other patients – at least they would not be mobbed, yet.

He moved another step closer to her and reached out a hand to touch her.

Matilda stepped back, trying not to move too quickly, as she had been warned that sudden moves frightened some patients.

She cleared her throat. 'Are you enjoying the garden?' she asked, her voice thin and high.

'You've come,' he said.

'My name is Matilda,' she said, hoping to make him realise she was not the person he was expecting. 'Let's sit and we'll talk,' she said and indicated the bench.

He put his head back and laughed. 'I knew you would come.'

Matilda glanced to the ladies, who were not aware of the threat, continuing with their pre-occupations.

He made a snatch for Matilda, and she gave a scream and stepped back, hitting the wall of the green maze behind her, trapped. His hand went to her face and neck, and she grasped it, attempting to push him away and stay calm.

'Let us sit,' she said again, terrified, as his grip tightened and he moved in close to her, blocking her vision of the ladies and the light from above. She tried to scream, but his grip was too tight, and now his free hand had found her waist and began moving up.

Suddenly he was gone, knocked to the ground by Thomas, with a threat to stay down. Matilda felt Thomas grab her, and he tucked her behind him. The man rose again, and Thomas ordered him down. The patient glared at Thomas and then collapsed into a ball and cried. All the tension left Thomas's body.

The uniformed orderlies rushed in, along with Harry and lifted the man, treating him with roughness.

Matilda caught Harry's eye and answered his question with a quick nod. She was all right, thanks to Thomas.

'Easy up, boys, he's not well, it's not his fault,' Harry said to the orderlies.

Matilda clutched Thomas's arm, needing the security of his presence and strength. She was breathing heavy, equally relieved and frightened.

They watched as the orderlies tried to restrain the crying patient who thrashed around, not wishing to go with them. Finally, he was under control.

'What the hell were you doing? Where were you?' Thomas shouted at them in anger.

The orderly on duty stumbled through an apology and disappeared as quickly as he came with the other orderlies, the patient bundled between them. Harry followed them to give Thomas a moment alone.

Matilda turned and whispered calming words to the ladies as best she could. Their eyes were enormous, watching the drama as if it were a stage play. She turned her attention to Thomas as he faced her and, despite propriety, she clung to him. She felt his hand on her back and gently on the back of her head, pressing her against his chest.

'You are safe,' he said, lowering himself slightly to look into her eyes.

Matilda choked back her tears. She was not one to cry, never had been especially growing up in the company of four brothers, but the shock had overridden that. He raised his head, placing his chin on the top of her head, tucking her to him, and holding her close.

After a brief time, Thomas asked, 'Are you all right?' He pulled away to look down at her face.

She nodded, her breathing still fast. 'I was terrified. Where did you come from?' she asked incredulously.

He gently ran his thumb over her cheek, wiping away a tear. 'Harry and I were upstairs hoping to see Dr O'Shea. Thank God we were. I don't want to think of what might have happened otherwise.'

She took a deep breath. 'I would have screamed, and help would have come, eventually.'

He scoffed. 'Not quickly enough. I don't want you here, Matilda,' he said firmly.

She swallowed and nodded. 'I know.'

'We will talk about this,' he added.

She nodded again. 'I need to get the ladies back inside.'

'I'll see you home; you've had a shock,' he said, not encouraging her to let go, but Matilda straightened and adjusted her dress and collar. She shook her head.

'Georgina is inside. We'll travel home together.'

Matilda allowed Thomas to escort her and the ladies inside, and with a promise to discuss later, he departed with Harry.

Despite the shock and the fear that was still swirling inside her, Matilda did not want to give up anything. But she resolved she needed to be stronger, to learn to fend for herself. To fight back.

Chapter 22

'So, tell me everything, Matilda. Did you find anything?' Georgina asked as they headed to the omnibus at the end of the tour and their volunteering efforts for the day. Georgina was not aware of what had happened, and Matilda did not wish to speak of it in detail.

But she had forgotten about their clandestine search with Elijah in the drama that had followed.

'Find?' she asked, confused.

'Yes, with your brother, in Meredith's sewing room?' Georgina asked, now a little bewildered by Matilda's response.

'Forgive me, I was in a slight incident in the garden, and I am a little rattled.'

'No! Are you okay? Should we sit for a moment?' Georgina asked. Matilda could feel her dear friend studying her.

'Thank you, but no. It was a male patient in the garden with me, Hannah and Kirra. He had wandered away from his work party, but fortunately nothing came of it.'

'Goodness,' Georgina said, her hand going to her heart. 'I am sure I would have struck out in fear.'

'That's what I want to do,' Matilda agreed. 'I don't want to be vulnerable. I must learn to protect myself.'

'Let us learn together,' Georgina concluded as they exited the gates of the asylum. 'Although I do have height on my side which I can use to my advantage.'

Matilda calmed herself, thinking back on how Georgina distracted Dr O'Shea and assisted herself and Elijah. 'How did you know what we were up to?' she asked with a smile.

Georgina tapped her nose. 'I sense these things. I always have. My father says I am quite intuitive – I know when calving is about to begin before the cow does sometimes,' she said and laughed at her own joke. 'But in all seriousness, as Meredith is your brother's patient, I assumed he would want to get to the bottom of the mystery of what made her want to jump. She'd been medicated, I imagine.'

'I don't know, but Elijah said he prescribed nothing that would bring on that kind of reaction.' Matilda lowered her voice, glanced around to ensure they could not be overhead and said, 'We found a drug bottle in her sewing kit.'

'No!'

'True. Elijah will need to determine what was in it, and who gave it to her.'

Georgina shook her head. 'Dreadful. Thank God we were spared the sight of that lovely woman falling.'

'We must keep it to ourselves though… my finding.'

'Absolutely!' Georgina declared. 'Who is to say who might be involved and we don't want to put anyone in danger.'

They hailed the omnibus as it drew closer.

'It's rather exciting, isn't it?' Georgina added, tucking her drawing pad under her arm as the ladies lifted their skirts slightly to step up on the rail.

Matilda grinned. 'I do love a good mystery.'

Once seated, Matilda smiled at Georgina and touched her arm. 'I think someone is a little charmed by you.'

Georgina scoffed. 'Oh, he always acts like that. I assure you Dr O'Shea thinks of me as a friend and nothing more. I think he might have had intentions once, but I've never reciprocated his feelings. He would be a rather exhausting partner, I imagine.'

Matilda hesitated, surprised, and Georgina's mouth formed an 'O'.

'You were not referring to Dr O'Shea, were you?' Georgina asked. She readjusted her hat, a little flustered.

'No.'

Georgina looked straight ahead. 'I scarcely hope to draw the attention of your handsome and clever brother. I am not a conventional beauty or charming or diplomatic – the type of lady I imagine your brother to have on his arm and need for his career advancement.'

Matilda smiled. 'Nonsense. You are many good things, including practical, sensible, amusing and handsome – wonderful traits for any ambitious man. I think he might be quite smitten with you.'

'Oh, wouldn't that be wonderful?' She turned to face Matilda. 'Goodness,' she said and could not help grinning. But then Georgina sobered. 'Would you think it was wonderful?' she asked, frowning at Matilda.

'Of course I would! It would thrill me to see you both find happiness with each other. Why would I not be happy?' Matilda asked, puzzled.

Georgina frowned at her. 'I am not every mother's first choice for their son, or sister's choice for their brother, for that matter. Some find me rather like a bull in a china shop.'

'Well, I assure you, I am not one of those. Besides, as I said to Alice, I have four sister-in-law positions and three available. If you and Alice could take two of those, I would be selfishly thrilled,' she said with a grin, reciprocated by Georgina.

'I have to show you something,' Georgina said. She opened her drawing folder and scanned through the pages.

'My you are an amazing illustrator,' Matilda said in awe of the drawings of the asylum and women that she caught brief glimpses of, and then there was Elijah. A full-page portrait of his face, neck high. Matilda looked from the drawing to Georgina.

'This is a beautiful likeness.' She studied her brother's square jaw, wide eyes and caring expression, even the handsome manner in which his necktie appeared and disappeared off the edge of the page. 'You have really captured his demeanour.'

'Yes, I had feelings for him the moment our eyes connected, but I never hoped,' Georgina said.

'You must show him this, Georgina, it is masterful.'

'Perhaps I will,' she said and shrugged. 'Unless you would like to take it home and show him.'

'Should I?' Matilda said with a smile. 'I doubt he needs any encouragement, but this will give him courage.'

Georgina laughed. 'I hardly believe he needs that either. He is, after all, the prize, not me.' She rolled it up, fetched a small red ribbon from her bag, tied it and handed it to Matilda.

'I shall report back on Elijah's reaction on Monday,' Matilda said, 'before our morning meeting.'

'Only tell me should he like it,' Georgina requested closing her drawing pad. 'I could not bear it otherwise. If he seems appalled, please do me the kindness of telling your brother that I painted many portraits, including those of the nurses and patients. That way he need not assume I have feelings for him or be embarrassed when he next encounters me.'

'I can tell you now,' Matilda said as her stop came into sight. 'I am sure it will make his day.' She carefully tucked the portrait in her bag, not expecting to have an audience with Elijah until Sunday, given he was working odd hours. But Matilda had no intention of leaving it in his room, as she wanted to see his reaction first-hand. With an exchange of goodbyes, Matilda alighted.

Hurrying home, she mused on Elijah's situation. She would be in his good books with the painting and the medicine bottle – a reciprocal favour for the volunteer opportunity. Matilda felt the need to see Thomas now to enjoy the thrill of her own romantic liaison.

Chapter 23

For Matilda and Mr Hayward – the two family members consistently at dinner most nights of the week in the Hayward household – it was always a surprise to see who would join them for Sunday lunch. Once, only the established family was in attendance, but now that all the children were adults and several with partners, it was shifting sands. What didn't change were the heads of the table and today was no different. Mr Hayward and his sister, Audrey, presided at each end overlooking the Hayward brood – all in their Sunday best.

Today Amos, the eldest Hayward son and Aunt Audrey's favourite nephew, was in attendance, along with his wife, Minnie. The young lawyer and his wife looked the part. Minnie was dressed in the finest fabric, and Amos worked hard to provide it for her. Daniel and Alice sat beside them, a lively and conversable couple. Daniel was quite taken by his pretty English love and accepted by her guardian to court her. Opposite were Matilda and Thomas, which was still a novelty for the family seeing the couple paired, although

Thomas had always been enamoured by Matilda. Elijah was there on his own, the handsome second-youngest male with a day off from his asylum posting. His twin, Gideon, was not in attendance.

As everyone took their seats and Thomas held the chair for Matilda, she waited until he was seated before whispering, 'We must talk about your case.'

'Must we?' he asked, not wanting to talk about work for the day. He attempted to change the subject, but Matilda continued. 'I imagine there are some interesting developments… I hear you have exhumed Mrs Hilda Rodgers?'

'How on earth did you hear that?' Thomas asked, a frustrated look across his countenance.

Matilda tapped her nose, and he shook his head and smiled at her.

'You are a spy, not a journalist,' he teased. 'So, I did tell you you look beautiful today, didn't I?'

'I'm sure you didn't!' she exclaimed. 'I would have remembered that.'

'Oh, right then,' he said and added nothing more. Matilda gave him an expectant look, and he laughed.

'As always, but particularly today, you look beautiful, Tillie.'

Matilda gave him a smile. 'Thank you, Thomas. It is nice to dress for church and Sunday lunch afterwards. My work day dresses are becoming much more practical.'

'I imagine necessity dictates,' Thomas said drily.

'Indeed, like the other day at the asylum when Georgina

and I had to race with the crowd to find out what the shouting was about at the side of the main building, it was good to be in less restricted skirts.'

Thomas sighed. 'I'm sure. Is that a new dress?'

Matilda looked down at her peach-coloured dress with cream lace and ran her hand along the delicate fabric, as Thomas longed to do.

'It is. Another gift from Aunt Audrey. She does spoil me,' Matilda said with an affectionate smile towards her aunt, who understood and reciprocated on seeing Matilda touching the fabric of her new dress.

'You are her only niece,' Thomas said, admiring Audrey's good taste.

Matilda lowered her voice and spoke nearer to Thomas's ear. He inclined to hear her. 'I suspect it is for your benefit. She likes you to see me looking feminine and pretty in the hope that you will whisk me away and make an honest woman of me.' Matilda smiled and moved away, taking Thomas's breath with her.

'Aunt Audrey is right. I love you looking like this, so beautiful and feminine.'

'And inquisitive?' she asked with a smile and a raised eyebrow. Matilda knew full well that he was not a fan of her occupation when it led to dangerous situations and, oddly, it seemed to be the case of late.

'Just as you are,' he said and took her hand and kissed it, with no self-consciousness in front of the family. It was part of his plan to ensure the Hayward family saw them as a couple, more so than seeing the boy who accepted them as his surrogate family.

Mr Hayward's voice broke through the conversations happening around the table. 'Lovely to have you all with us again today and welcome again, Alice. We are so glad you are joining us regularly,' he said. 'Of course, Minnie, you need no special welcome as you are family, as is Thomas.'

'Legally in Minnie's case,' Amos added with a smile, as it was his line of business. 'Whereas Thomas is family by default, and Alice, well, we live in hope that you will take Daniel off our hands.'

Alice laughed with delight, and Daniel smiled and nudged her.

'Where is your twin brother today, Elijah?' Aunt Audrey asked.

'Gideon sends his apologies, Aunt. Miss Lily Chappell and her family have asked him to lunch.'

'Lunch with Miss Chappell,' Matilda said with surprise. 'Are you okay with that, Elijah?'

'Why wouldn't he be?' Aunt Audrey snapped. 'Elijah doesn't expect his twin to be by his side forever, surely. You have been away at medical school for several years and both of you appear to have borne the separation.'

'I assure you, Aunt Audrey, I do not covet my twin's company around the clock,' Elijah said with a laugh.

Daniel explained. 'Miss Chappell had set her sights on Elijah before he artfully dodged her, and she met Gideon.'

'Oh, is that so?' Aunt Audrey asked with a raised eyebrow in Elijah's direction. 'That was a very clever pun, Daniel. Congratulations to you. Especially as Gideon runs an art gallery.'

'Thank you, Aunt Audrey, for appreciating my brilliance. Not everybody does,' Daniel joked and bore the jests that followed.

Aunt Audrey continued. 'Elijah, you could do worse. If I have my Chappells correct, her father is an engineer, is he not? I met a Mr Chappell at a council committee meeting and I believe he mentioned a daughter of age.'

'That is him, Aunt Audrey. But I am very grateful Miss Chappell has transferred her interest to Gideon,' Elijah assured the family. 'I think her penchant for never-ending outings and amusements would be beyond my capacity to uphold. Gideon, on the other hand, would like nothing better.'

'Then we must find someone worthy of you, Elijah,' Aunt Audrey said, pursing her lips as she thought about a list of applicants.

Matilda grinned at her brother, delighted to not be the centre of Aunt Audrey's marital and matchmaking tendencies for one day. She nudged Thomas, and he gave her a look that suggested she should not be too cocky just yet.

'Thank you, Aunt Audrey, but I believe I may have met someone who is quite fascinating,' Elijah admitted.

'Really?' Daniel turned to his younger brother. 'And you are prepared to admit it here and bear the never-ending questions and pushes to secure her?'

The family laughed as the routine was all too familiar, and Thomas received several looks and nudges which he bore in good grace.

'I thought it might save time,' Elijah said in jest.

'So, son, who is this lovely woman as I've no doubt you would only be attracted to someone genuine?' Mr Hayward asked.

Elijah hesitated. 'I am not sure she reciprocates my feelings yet, Pa, so it is too early to say. But I assure you all, should I pursue the matter, everyone here will be the second to know. The young lady being the first.'

'I believe she does care for you, Elijah,' Matilda said.

Alice's eyes widened. 'Do you know this fortunate lady, Matilda?'

'I believe I do, isn't that so?' she said with a smile to Elijah, who rolled his eyes and gave a curt nod. She refrained from telling Alice that she knew Elijah's love interest, too.

'But it not for me to tell,' Matilda continued. 'I do have a small gift from her to you,' Matilda said and despite Elijah's look of happiness and embarrassment, and the family's harassment to know more, Matilda held her ground and revealed nothing.

'Hear, hear,' Aunt Audrey said. 'Now that is how it is done, Matilda. So how are you two progressing?' she said with a look at Thomas and her niece.

Matilda's grimace drew a round of laughs. But fortunately, the serving of lunch and handing around of plates provided a reprieve from responding for the moment.

'What a week of news it has been,' Matilda said, hoping to change the subject. 'Don't you agree, Pa?'

'Quite so,' he said. 'The burning down of the beautiful Exhibition Building…' he looked to his sister, Audrey, who tutted on cue.

'There's been an intriguing case in the court of a great swindle. It's been challenging keeping up with the demand for court illustrations,' Daniel said, reflecting on his week.

'I cannot believe I had two clients seeking matrimonial divorce suits this week,' Amos shared, and Minnie shook her head and added, 'both married in a church as well!'

'At the *Women's Journal* we've been reporting on the Washington Conference of Women that has brought together so many important voices and issues,' Alice added with enthusiasm.

'And I have been commissioned to write several articles about women at the asylum; perhaps it will make people more sympathetic. Just this week at least one woman was saved from falling to her death thanks to Elijah,' Matilda said with a glance to her brother, but noting Aunt Audrey's sigh and shake of the head at Matilda's choice of a news event. She felt Thomas stiffen beside her and, soon after when small groups of conversation formed, he turned to Elijah.

'What was that about a woman attempting to jump at the asylum? Is that recent?' Thomas asked. Until now he had been happy to relax knowing that a group of this size and his familiarity among it, required him to contribute very little and he could enjoy Cook's splendid lunchtime meal.

Matilda elaborated. 'Elijah bravely talked one of his patients away from the window when she insisted she had grown wings and was going to try them.'

'Her first flight,' Elijah explained. 'To date, Meredith has been such a sedate and calm patient. But fortunately, she didn't get the chance to fly… the orderlies restrained her.'

Thomas frowned. 'Hilda Rodgers's last word was "fly". Odd given she too, spent time at the asylum where you have been appointed, Elijah. Is flying a normal preoccupation of the insane?'

'Not that I am aware of, but I am a novice at asylum life and did not specialise in mannerisms of the insane during my studies,' Elijah said. 'But Thom, I intended to mention something to you in case it warranted it down the track.'

'Please do,' Thomas said, leaning forward slightly to hear Elijah's words.

'Straight after Meredith's attempted flight, I went to her aid and on her breath, I could smell laudanum. I did not administer it.'

Thomas froze, his eyes narrowed. 'Twice in a matter of days I have come across that drug and both somehow related to patients, or former patients, of the asylum.'

'So then, that was the contents of the dropper bottle you mentioned at Wednesday night dinner?' Elijah asked, before passing the bread as requested by Daniel.

'Yes. It was laudanum inside, but not a trace of it in the victim's body – Raymond Rodgers. We have exhumed Mrs Rodgers' body to test it and we've checked their sons' alibis.'

Matilda gave a small gasp and Thomas's eyes widened.

'Not a word Matilda, promise me? That is police to doctor talk,' Thomas warned.

'Why can't it be police to doctor to journalist talk?' she asked, and then, seeing Thomas's worried expression, she smiled. 'Do not worry, I promise it will go no further. I don't rush off and publish every word you say.'

'Praise the Lord for that,' Thomas said with a sigh, and Elijah chuckled.

Matilda glanced to Aunt Audrey, and satisfied she was still in conversation with Minnie and Amos, lowered her voice to say, 'There is more; tell Thomas about your searches, Elijah.' She nudged him, and Elijah mentioned the window bars and the sewing room find.

'Matilda assisted me in searching Meredith's sewing room where we found a small bottle of laudanum in her sewing kit. Again, I did not administer this.'

'Can you not keep out of trouble?' Thomas asked, looking at Matilda and rolling his eyes. 'Can I have the bottle?' he asked Elijah.

'I have it here. I'll give it to you before you depart today.'

Matilda added: 'Did you hear what that doctor said to you after they pulled Meredith from the window? Who was he, Elijah?'

'That's my counterpart, Dr Victor McQuade. He looks after the men's ward,' Elijah told Matilda and Thomas.

Thomas nodded. 'What did he say?'

Matilda answered. 'Just one word – "Criminal" – and then he walked off.'

'Who was he talking to or about?' Thomas asked.

Elijah gave a small shrug. 'He was looking up at the window, then he shook his head, muttered the word and left. It could have meant any number of things. It was criminal that the bars were not on the windows, or that Meredith was administered or not administered with drugs that might bring about her need to fly, or perhaps he thought it was criminal that she was prevented from jumping, but I highly doubt that given he is a doctor and that would be against his oath.'

They proceed to eat for a few moments while Thomas mused, eyes narrowed, thoughts going productively through his head. Then he asked, 'What do you know of Dr McQuade?'

'Absolutely nothing, other than he is surly and has – according to Dr O'Shea – much to improve with his bedside manner. However, I have enjoyed the small amount of time I have spent in his companionship. Dr O'Shea is the opposite and can be somewhat overbearing.' Elijah thought out loud, 'Meredith told Dr O'Shea she was ready to jump, as if he had been preparing her.'

'What can we do to assist, Thomas?' Matilda asked in all seriousness. 'I wish I could go undercover like Nellie Bly did and see if I could find out what was going on at the asylum, but the staff knows my face now.'

'Trust me, Matilda, that would never happen. Never. Over my dead body,' Thomas said with finality, amazed after the recent incident in the garden that she would even consider it.

'And mine after that,' Elijah agreed.

Matilda sighed and gave both men a frustrated look.

'Who is this Nellie Bly?' Elijah asked, looking up to pass the gravy boat as requested by Amos at the other end of the table.

'I'm surprised you don't remember her name,' Matilda said. 'Surely she has been spoken about in medical circles here?'

Elijah shook his head.

'She's amazing,' Matilda gushed. 'Nellie is a journalist who went undercover in a New York City insane asylum last year to reveal what really went on. It was terribly risky; she may not have been released. But when she was, her tales were harrowing.'

'It's insane,' Thomas said before realising what he said. 'I guess she fitted right in.'

Matilda gave him a wry look. 'For my part, should I have some subtle talks with the patients while I am volunteering?'

'No, it's too dangerous,' Thomas and Elijah both said, talking over each other.

Matilda rolled her eyes. 'No more dangerous than it is for both of you prodding and poking about in there.'

'It's a lot more dangerous,' Thomas said.

'How?' she asked.

'Just because,' Elijah said firmly, and the three of them grinned.

'What are you three whispering and laughing about down that end of the table?' Aunt Audrey asked, not being one to be left out of the conversation.

Matilda responded honestly. 'Elijah was just doing his best impression of Pa explaining why we couldn't do something when we were young ones.'

'Oh?' Mr Hayward said with a grin. 'Let's see it then.'

'Two words,' Elijah said, and his siblings caught on. In unison, Elijah, Daniel and Matilda responded; 'Just because!'

Mr Hayward laughed heartily. 'Well, it was good enough reason.'

The banter continued between the eating and drinking, and Thomas looked to Matilda.

'Thank you for the information about Meredith and what the doctor said. Yet again you have been wonderfully insightful,' he said giving praise where praise was due. 'But please put your safety above all else. As much as I would love to be your shield, I cannot be with you around the clock.'

She smiled and touched his leg under the table, unaware she caused him no end of pleasure and discomfort and not hearing the low groan he swallowed.

'I promise to take care,' she assured him. But to herself, she vowed to find out more and involve Georgina too if she was up for a cloak and dagger adventure.

Chapter 24

After Sunday lunch and before Thomas and Matilda enjoyed their customary afternoon walk with Daniel and Alice, Matilda hurried to her room to retrieve Georgina's drawing for Elijah. She slipped it to him privately as they met in the hallway between their rooms. Elijah was not one for grandstanding.

'I shall open it later,' he said.

'But you can't,' Matilda implored him. 'I promised Georgina I would tell her of your reaction – if you like it or dislike it.'

'How could I not like it if she took the time to sketch me?' he asked.

'Georgina was mindful of being too forward. She did not wish for you to feel obligate to reply,' Matilda said. 'She is refreshingly natural.'

'I could not agree more,' Elijah said and smiled at his sister.

Matilda heard Thomas's voice drifting up the stairs as he spoke with Daniel in their familiar, relaxed manner. She returned her attention to Elijah as he looked at the rolled-up paper, and leaning on the upstairs railing, slipped the red ribbon from it. Matilda noticed he pocketed the ribbon. Elijah unrolled it and his breath hitched.

'My, she is very talented, isn't she?' he said, his eyes taking in every inch of the portrait.

'I think she has captured you perfectly,' Matilda said, watching him. 'It's a very handsome portrait.'

He gave a small smile and rolled it up, regaining his composure. 'Please tell Miss Urry that I thought it was exceptional, and I am most grateful.'

Matilda put her hand on his arm. 'Elijah, it is Georgina you speak of? The lady who interests you, isn't it? I do not wish to give her false encouragement.'

'Yes, it is. She is quite extraordinary, and now…' he said, waving the rolled-up portrait at Matilda, 'I shall act upon it.'

She smiled with delight, kissed him on the cheek and hurried downstairs where Thomas, Daniel and now Alice awaited.

*****

Thomas ensured they walked far enough behind Daniel and Alice so that he could have some privacy with Matilda. He would prefer if no one accompanied them at all, but at least Daniel was too preoccupied with Alice to care what his best friend and sister were up to.

'I do not get to see you often enough,' he began, hoping his intentions and direction of the conversation would soon become clear. 'There is not one moment of the day when I do not think of you.'

'You are busy, and I understand that,' she replied and smiled, not saying what he wanted to hear or needed to hear. Would she be more effusive with a lover who entered her life now and not a suitor she had always known? Thomas was never really sure of the depths of Matilda's feelings for him, and he was fairly confident they did not extend to the depths he felt.

He looked away, frustrated, and tried again. 'I am sure I saw more of you when we were younger, than now that we are courting.'

Matilda smiled up at him. 'Well, since Daniel is not home to play with you anymore, there is probably truth in that.'

He smiled at her, knowing she was teasing him, but it was not what he needed this afternoon. Another week of death and insanity had made him realise how much he wanted normality – a life with Matilda, a wife to come home to, children that they raised as a family – the home life he never had growing up.

He felt the weight of her small hand on his arm and struggled with the desire to kiss her there and then in public. She ran a finger along a scar on his wrist.

'What is troubling you?' she asked.

He frowned and looked ahead, thinking about his words. Matilda said his name, and he looked down upon her face, slowing their stride.

'I know you as well as I know myself, Thomas. Say what bothers you,' she said.

He was conscious of appearing weak in her presence and did not want to beg for the state of her affection, and so he couched his words obliquely, hoping they conveyed his meaning.

'All week I see horrors and cruelty, and then I think of you and want to protect you and hold you. I want to see your face and feel your touch,' he said and glanced away, embarrassed. 'It is calming for me,' he added, returning his gaze to her.

Thomas suspected Matilda did not understand what role she was to play now that he had declared his emotions. Society dictated the ball was in his court, but he did not think she was ready for a proposal yet.

In front of him, Daniel turned to call something back and Thomas gave him a frown and a quick shake of his head. Daniel nodded and turned back, pointing at something in the distance to show Alice. Thomas resolved to be direct. He was very much off balance with the conversation going around in his head and the quicker it was said, the better.

'I want to be married sooner rather than later.' He glanced at her for a reaction but hurried on. 'With your consent, I will speak to your father about it. Unless you would like some time to consider what I am suggesting?' He feared her rejection. Feared that she might ask for a long courtship and felt anxious about what that might mean.

'You are saying you do not want a long courtship?' Matilda asked directly.

'Yes, Tillie, that is what I am saying.' He cleared his throat of emotion. 'I want to be together as husband and wife as soon as possible.'

'Hmm. So, you are saying that you can't live without me and want me as your wife immediately,' she said and looked at him with a straight face and then laughed lightly at his wry expression.

Thomas rolled his eyes. 'Yes, summed up perfectly,' he said and smiled as she laughed.

'Forgive me, Thomas. I don't wish to make fun of your sincerity. Know that I am very touched and flattered by your words,' she said and looked away. 'But have you really thought this through?' she asked and surprised him.

'Of course. It has taken up many hours of my day and night, of that you can be assured.'

She walked on with him in silence for a few moments and then said: 'You will be giving up your independent life. Instead of having the freedom to go to your club and hotel or wherever you frequent, you will have a woman at home waiting for you,' she pointed out. 'Instead of the kisses of wanton women, you will have to resign yourself to one woman kissing you.' Matilda wore a challenging expression.

He studied the beautiful form of his beloved Matilda. He looked at her lips and then moved his gaze to his eyes. For a moment she appeared to raise herself to lean into him, waiting for his response. His body stiffened with her closeness.

'That is exactly what I want,' he said and then added drily. 'Assuming you are home when I arrive.' She laughed at his condescension towards her career.

'Then what are you waiting for?' Matilda asked, and Thomas took a moment to realise what she said before he smiled and looked away, flushed with relief.

'My only concern…' she said, and Thomas's heart stopped, 'is Pa.'

Thomas nodded. 'Your father will still have Elijah, Gideon and Daniel coming in and out at different times and we could dine with him mid-week, as well as Sunday, if that abated any concerns you might have?'

'Yes, that would make me feel better, and of course I will probably be there more than you since you'll be kept at work a great deal. But Thomas…'

'Yes?' he asked, prepared to agree to anything at this stage.

'I want a formal proposal,' she said. 'Do not think this discussion substitutes for one.'

'I wouldn't dream of it,' he said, taking her request on board.

'I want something romantic that I can tell our children about one day when they ask how Daddy proposed to Mummy.'

Thomas smiled with pleasure; a smile that soon faded as she continued.

'And something I can tell my friends, colleagues and brothers when they ask how you proposed because they are bound to ask, especially the ladies.'

Thomas grimaced at the thought of the ribbing he would incur at the hands of Matilda's brothers – his close friends. She nudged him when he did not respond quickly enough.

'I assure you, Tillie, I will do my best to make it romantic,' he said.

On hearing a child clapping, they both looked towards

the pond as two ducks landed with grace and received the ovation from a delighted family.

'They'll be good looking, our children,' Thomas teased, and Matilda laughed.

'You know twins run in my family,' she warned him. 'Best you make inspector sooner rather than later.'

He laughed. In front, Daniel and Alice turned to return and walked towards them. Thomas looked at Daniel and gave a smile and nod.

*****

When they caught up, Matilda introduced a new subject.

'I discovered from the international newspapers that Alice is receiving, that women in London are taking self-defence classes.' Matilda did not need to look at Thomas to know what his expression might be and a glance at Daniel confirmed he knew better than to laugh at matters related to women and their independence, especially in the company of Alice.

Alice continued. 'It is true. Women are fighting back and protecting themselves against mashers,' she said.

'Mashers?' Daniel asked, having not heard the term.

Thomas answered. 'A man who makes unwelcomed advances,' he said and cleared his throat, leaving it at that.

'Precisely so,' Alice answered, as the handsome paired couples neared the end of the park to head for home.

'And you are intending to take up lessons in this art, Tillie?' Thomas asked, adding, 'I am not entirely averse to the idea given the dangerous situations you put yourself in.'

'Hear, hear,' Daniel agreed. 'You should take some lessons too, Alice, especially if you intend to remain in close company with my sister.'

'Oh, I intend to,' she said with an engaging smile to Daniel, which made him grin. Thomas rolled his eyes and Matilda laughed.

'I have found no one locally who knows of an instructor, but I found some drawings with instructions, and I have been practising for the last night or two,' Matilda said, her head held high. 'One has to know her limitations though, and I know that some of the suggested defences in the drawings I could not achieve.'

'Well, give us a demonstration,' Thomas said, stopping in a small, private garden area and moving a little away from Matilda so she could show them her new skills.

'You are just making fun of me, Thomas,' she said, looking up at him, her eyes narrowing.

'I am doing nothing of the sort. I would be happy to assist where possible,' he said, merriment on his face and Daniel gave a grin, knowing his best friend only too well. 'You may use me as your assailant. Lord knows you have many times in the past when I've least expected it.'

Matilda smiled at the memory of her unforeseen attacks on her brothers and Thomas when revenge called for it.

'Do show us, Matilda,' Alice begged. 'I would be keen to receive some tips.'

She nodded. 'Very well, but what if I hurt you, Thomas? I will feel bad, and you will be in pain. Perhaps I'd best practise on my pillow.'

Daniel spoke up. 'The best type of training is from the real thing… same with boxing,' he said with a glance to Thomas.

'True, you learn the techniques quickly when you are knocked out a few times,' Thomas agreed. 'Come then, Tillie, let's begin.' He slipped off his jacket and hat and passed them to Daniel. Running a hand through his hair and preparing himself, Thomas came to stand opposite her. 'Shall I move as if I am threatening you?'

Matilda moved closer to Thomas, positioned herself, and invited him to do so. She did not remove her dainty straw hat with the black band and flower pin, nor concern herself with dirtying her peach-coloured dress with the cream lace. Matilda raised her hands into fists. Thomas grinned.

'Thomas, you are being most unhelpful,' she scolded him.

'I am sorry, but you look so adorable,' he said and smiled warmly at her. 'Such a cute little fist.'

'I am not intending to look adorable. This is menacing,' she said, and Alice giggled.

'Oh, sorry,' Alice added quickly, trying to remove the smile from her face, 'but you do look rather sweet.'

Matilda frowned at the three of them and Daniel held up his hands.

'I did not say a thing,' he assured her and when Matilda gave him a grateful look he added, 'but I was thinking it.'

The group laughed and Matilda gave a scolding look to each of them. 'I know I have little chance of fighting back if Thomas were to rush me, but there are some things I can do.'

Thomas refocused. 'Right then. So, you are going to use the skills that you think will best serve you,' he continued, 'and a fist fight is what you are thinking? Throw me a punch then.'

She did so, and he grabbed her hand and kissed the top of it. Matilda pulled her hand away.

'Thomas! Unless you expect my attacker to do the same, that is most impractical.'

'I certainly hope they do not,' he said sharply. 'Although it is a better alternative to them attacking you, of course. I might show more mercy on them in that case.'

Matilda ignored his possessiveness, took a deep breath and stood to full height, which came only to Thomas and Daniel's shoulders. 'I am warning you now to be on your guard as I intend to use one of the few skills I have with my size and strength.'

'I can't wait to see this,' Daniel said, and Alice nudged him in good fun.

'Consider me on guard,' Thomas said. 'Shall I lunge?'

'When you are ready,' she said.

Thomas smiled at her and circled for a moment. Matilda could hear Daniel chuckling and a glance at Alice confirmed she was studying with much interest for her own learning.

'Don't smile, Thomas. It does not make you look very menacing,' she told him.

'I do not want to frighten you,' he said with concern.

Matilda rolled her eyes, and he vowed to do better. And then as Thomas neared, Matilda threw her small fist towards his face. Thomas went to grab her hand again, but not before Matilda gave him a swift and hard kick in the kneecap.

'Ouch!' he yelled, jumping back, bending over and rubbing his knee.

'Ah-ha! There you have it,' she exclaimed, victorious. 'Now if you were really my attacker, I would give you a good push over while you leaned forward or run as fast as I could while you were hobbled.' She smiled at all three and looked particularly pleased with herself.

Thomas rubbed his knee.

'Are you all right, Thom?' Daniel teased and earned a smirk.

'I shall live,' he said, pretending to limp.

'I am sorry, Thomas,' Matilda said, looking worried, 'but I did warn you.'

'Best you stay close to help me home then,' he said with a wink to Daniel on retrieving his coat and hat.

'I saw that,' she told him, and Thomas laughed.

He donned his jacket and hat, and moving as close as propriety allowed, walked behind his best friend and Miss Alice Doran, to take his beloved Matilda home.

Chapter 25

Matilda sat opposite her editor, waiting for the verdict on her second asylum-related submission for the *Women's Journal* and watching as her editor read it. She was in awe of Mrs Lawson and hoped to be just like her one day – printing the written word, encouraging young writers and being part of the fabric of her community. Married to Thomas too, of course, and with a family. A girl could have it all if she tried hard enough – it was 1888, after all.

Now and then Mrs Lawson's eyes widened, or she smile or nodded with sadness. Each time, Matilda died a thousand deaths waiting for the verdict. Finally, Mrs Lawson looked up.

'Exceptional,' Mrs Lawson proclaimed.

Matilda's mouth dropped open in surprise. 'Really, Mrs Lawson?'

'Yes, really. This is excellent work. Passionate, interesting, sympathetic, well done, Matilda, your best work yet,' Mrs Lawson said. 'Although I thought the piece you wrote on the artist's muse was also very good.'

'Thank you. I am so relieved,' Matilda said, her hand going to her heart which had resumed beating normally. 'They are the most torrid tales.'

'It makes you realise how lucky we are,' Mrs Lawson agreed. 'One more week at the asylum for you and Georgina, and then we'll put you on a different story. You can continue to volunteer in your own time, of course.'

'I shall do. Thank you, Mrs Lawson. It has been so wonderful to work with Georgina; she has truly captured the soul of the women on her page.'

'Yes, I fear we may lose her to the country soon though. She is restless,' Mrs Lawson said with a glance out the large glass window of her office to the ladies at work and Georgina in the far corner. She removed her glasses and sat back, folding her hands on the table in front of her and studying Matilda.

'Breaking no confidences, have you upturned anything that might assist your beau in his investigation, or have they deemed Mrs Rodgers death a suicide?' Mrs Lawson asked.

'I believe the investigation is still open, mainly because there appears to be a rash of people choosing to jump of late,' Matilda said, 'more than usual at the asylum I was told by one of the orderlies. Also, Mr Rodgers' killer has not yet been found.'

'A terrible state of affairs for that poor family.' She waved the rest of the staff in as they made their way to her office for the morning meeting.

'Keep up the good work, dear,' she said with a smile to Matilda.

'I will do my best and thank you, Mrs Lawson,' Matilda said, rising and moving down the table to sit with her casual staff colleagues.

She couldn't be happier. Her story was about to be published and part of it included a clue that she thought might be very valuable to Thomas, if he had not already taken that line of thinking – Meredith, like Mrs Hilda Rodgers – was still married. Was the seamstress worth more dead than alive?

*****

Women's Journal
Tuesday, 24 July 1888
Fortnightly edition Vol.1, No.19.
Price, 3d.

The lady of the sewing room – Meredith of the asylum

A short series presenting an exclusive insight into life for women at the Asylum for the Insane at Wacol. Report by Matilda Hayward. Illustration by Georgina Urry.

--oOo--

In the corner of a sewing room sits a

refined lady in her middle years. Tall and softly spoken, a stiff-collared uniform grey dress does not hide her attractiveness but accentuates her high cheekbones. A beauty in her youth, graceful in her maturity.

'I have always had a talent for sewing. My mother and grandmother were both renowned seamstresses in my hometown of Newcastle Upon Tyne,' Mrs Meredith Martineau says.

'When I met my beloved husband, Earl, he encouraged me to maintain my work. He was a builder's labourer, so the extra income allowed us to save for a home. We had grand plans.'

Meredith smiled and looked away as she remembered their youthful years, dreams and plans.

'He's coming for me soon,' Meredith added. 'He's away working at the building site, and I am managing the shop.'

But this is not a normal sewing room and shop, and this is not a normal seamstress. Mrs Meredith Martineau is the seamstress at the Asylum for the Insane, and herself a resident. But that was not always the case.

Despite his strong work ethic, the building industry did not provide a stable income for Earl and his new bride, and thus, the couple accepted assisted immigration to Australia to start a new life.

'We sailed on the *Glen Isla* and luckily we were both of hearty stock. Not everyone survived the journey,' Meredith recalled. 'We settled in a few towns before deciding on Brisbane. We hadn't counted on the fire.'

It was nearly 20 years ago to the day, when Meredith, then 22, along with 10 other ladies, were trapped in a millinery factory as flames tore through the building.

Meredith does not recall what happened except to say there was a fire and she was marked. History tells us that initially, only two ladies survived, but the other seamstress lost her fight and only Meredith remained to remember them. Her burns are extensive but hidden now by the dress that covers all but her face and hands, which remain unscarred. The lady of the sewing room, Meredith, has a great fear of heat and flame, as one might expect.

She begins work in the sewing room daily at 9am and closes the 'shop' at 4pm. All the uniforms and patients' clothing is made on-site by Meredith, assisted by several of the ladies competent in the craft. She is - all agree - highly skilled.

But be it fear, anxiety or melancholy, Meredith remains in the year of the fire, in her twenties and unable to move forward. Some nights she screams as if her body is on fire, other days she is confused and anticipates her beloved will propose soon and they will talk of a wedding and family.

Her parents have long since passed away. Her husband, Earl, is not coming. He returned to England many years ago.

Chapter 26

Thomas waited anxiously in the hallway of the Hayward household. Next to him, delaying his mission, was a young man who had delivered papers for Mr Hayward's signature from Amos, who had taken over his father's practice. Thomas and the young man politely exchanged a greeting and Thomas declined a cup of tea from Harriet. His partner, Detective Dart, was taking Mrs Dart to a medical practitioner this morning, and after this duty, Thomas intended to go straight to the coroner for Mrs Hilda Rodgers' results.

There was no need to be anxious, Thomas knew it, but still, it was a duty that filled him with trepidation, lest the unexpected should happen. The study door opened and Mr Hayward, resplendent as always, appeared.

'Thomas, forgive me for keeping you waiting. Do come in,' Mr Hayward said, handing the documents to the young man with his thanks. He shook hands with Thomas and the men entered his office and sat by the fireplace. It wasn't lit, but to sit at the desk seemed too formal.

'I'm sorry to keep you. I know duty beckons,' Mr Hayward said.

'That is of no consequence,' Thomas assured him. 'Work always beckons and I have a more important matter to discuss, one worth waiting for, I assure you.'

'Is everything all right?' Mr Hayward asked.

Thomas cleared his throat and nodded. 'Everything is fine, thank you, Mr Hayward. I would like to speak with you about Matilda.'

'Ah yes. Is your courtship progressing well?' he asked with a smile.

'Very well,' Thomas answered with a reciprocal smile he could not hide – a smile that came to his face whenever he thought of Matilda. He took a deep breath. 'I would like your permission please to ask for Matilda's hand now.' And then he waited, not moving, not breathing.

Mr Hayward nodded his understanding as if he always expected it to be so. Then he said, 'So soon?'

'I know it will be a loss to you to have her gone from your household, but I assure you she will be home regularly,' Thomas responded. 'I have learned in my role that one should grab with both hands, that which is good and protect it.'

Mr Hayward's look was one of melancholy, no doubt remembering the premature death of his wife. 'I've learned that lesson too, the hard way. You have discussed this with Matilda?' Mr Hayward asked.

'Yes, she is happy to progress our relationship, and I told her I would seek your blessing,' Thomas said anxiously.

He fidgeted, then stopped, remembering how his partner, Harry, said it showed impatience, not discipline.

Mr Hayward nodded. 'Fear not, Son, I am not averse to my own company or keeping my own house. I suspect there will always be one or two of the brood in and out. My only concern is for what is best for both of you, as you are like one of my own to me, Thom.'

'Thank you, sir,' Thomas answered, a lump rising in his throat.

Mr Hayward took a deep breath. 'If it were anyone else, Thomas, I would ask that the courtship be longer, maybe up to a year. But given you and Matilda have grown up together, I suspect you are most familiar with each other. However, friendship and relationships are two different things. But I've no doubt there is genuine affection between you both.'

'I love your daughter, Mr Hayward, I have all my life. I would do anything for her, give my life for hers in a heartbeat,' Thomas said.

Mr Hayward nodded. 'I know you would, as I've known you nearly all your life, Thomas. If you are both happy to bind your lives together, then by all means you have my blessing.'

Thomas exhaled and smiled. He looked up at Mr Hayward, who returned his grin, and then Thomas studied his future father-in-law. 'Did Matilda tell you I would be calling on this matter?'

Mr Hayward laughed. 'Of course, but what would be the fun of revealing that?'

Thomas chuckled.

'Besides, with only one daughter, I will only ever have one young man calling on me to ask for my daughter's hand in marriage, so I wanted to enjoy it. Which I did,' he confessed with a smile, which Thomas reciprocated. The men rose and shook hands again.

'I shall look forward to hearing all about it when the deed is done,' Mr Hayward said.

'Yes, that will be my next challenge. Something romantic but not over-the-top, something memorable but not fussy…'

Mr Hayward nodded. 'She's a tricky one, our Matilda.'

'I know it, but I am up for the challenge,' Thomas said with a grin, and after another round of enthusiastic thanks, he headed off to get his day started, the most challenging part now secured and accomplished.

Chapter 27

'My name is not really Birdie,' the little woman told Matilda and Georgina as she greeted them both early that afternoon. She ran her hands down her grey frock as if settling her feathers. Since the first day that Matilda began to work with Birdie to tell her story, Birdie could not continue, unable to recall any further details of her life. And so Matilda helped her, and other patients write letters and cards home or create simple poetry and verse.

'What is your real name then?' Georgina asked as they made their way to the painting easels, greeting the ladies and volunteers on their way.

'Ava. It means bird. I am like a bird, little and feathery, and my father used to call me Birdie. But I don't fly, I never fly, even if they try to make me.'

'That's a very pretty name,' Georgina said.

'And you are very sensible not attempting to fly. Nor do I,' Matilda agreed, as Birdie settled into a seat next to Georgina and several of the ladies. 'Surely no one tries to make you fly?' Matilda asked softly so that Winifred, the volunteer manager, did not hear.

Birdie nodded and looked very serious. 'They have told me I can, but I don't think so.'

'Who told you?' Georgina asked, with a glance to Matilda.

'It's a secret,' Birdie said, all solemnly.

The ladies got their charges started on this afternoon's projects and, as they had both agreed earlier, they would do their best to subtly get to the bottom of the matter of Meredith's attempt to fly out the window.

Matilda heard Georgina trying to get the secret from Birdie, saying in a sing-song voice. 'I bet it is not Dr Hayward who wants you to fly.'

'No,' Birdie agreed. 'He's very handsome. He said he has a sweetheart.'

Georgina caught Matilda's eye, and they exchanged a small smile.

'Isn't she a lucky girl?' Georgina said.

Before they could go any further with their sleuthing, the man in question entered the room with his assistant, the kind and matronly Nurse Kate.

'Good morning, Dr Hayward, Nurse Kate, are you both well on this fine day?' Winifred asked, delighted to see them.

'Never better, thank you, Winifred,' Elijah said and enquired the same of Winifred. Unlike Dr O'Shea, he did not call out a loud greeting to all, but wandered around to each patient greeting them and the volunteers, and individually checking on the patients' health.

Eventually, after many glances between himself and Miss Urry, as noted by Matilda, Elijah arrived by Matilda and Georgina's side of the room.

'Hello Matilda,' he said, sitting beside his sister to check on Rose – a confused young woman who loved to write poetry, although little of it made sense. Matilda thought her brother looked particularly handsome this afternoon. Perhaps it was the presence of Georgina in the same room that seemed to lift his spirits.

'Now Rose, you were feeling poorly yesterday… how is your stomach today?' Elijah asked.

'Much better, thank you, Doctor,' she said. 'The medicine helped, and I didn't eat any more grass.'

'Excellent,' he answered. 'Remember, you are not a rabbit, even though you do wiggle your nose like one.'

She giggled and showed Matilda, who laughed with delight.

'You are very good at bunny impersonations, Rose,' Matilda said. 'How clever you are.'

Elijah gave his sister a wink and moved on to Birdie and Georgina. He moved a collection of paintings from a chair to sit down beside Birdie.

'Miss Urry, Birdie, good day to you both,' he said.

'Doctor,' Georgina said and smile. 'We were just discussing secrets, weren't we, Birdie?'

'Yes, and I said I can't tell mine,' the little woman said with great seriousness.

'Rightly so,' Elijah said, but then saw Georgina shake her head slightly and he added. 'Although we could share a secret and I wouldn't tell.' He glanced to Nurse Kate who busied herself elsewhere.

'Me either,' Georgina said. 'I'm very good at keeping

secrets. When I am on the farm, the sheep often tell me things about the cows, but I never tell,' she joked, and Birdie clapped her hands with delight.

Elijah moved closer to her. 'If you keep that up, I may have to admit you,' he said and smiled.

'I'll advise the sheep no more secrets then,' she said, and he chuckled.

Matilda saw him glance her way, so she dropped her gaze even though she was too nearby not to overhear.

Birdie announced, 'I shall tell my secret but don't tell the sheep… promise?'

'I promise!' Georgina said with great sincerity. 'They won't get it out of me.'

'I am learning to fly!'

Matilda glanced up; her eyes wide with alarm. Georgina masked her shocked expression, saying 'Imagine that. Who is teaching you, as I might wish to learn too?'

'The angels,' the small woman said.

Elijah cleared his throat and said kindly but firmly: 'Birdie, you are not to fly without seeing me first and getting an official certificate, otherwise your wings won't work. Do you understand?' he said kindly, not wishing to frighten her.

'The certificate,' she said and nodded.

'Yes, you get one when you are ready. It's very important,' he said.

'And a great honour,' Georgina added solemnly, 'but you can't fly without one, absolutely not.'

'So come to see me when you are ready. There is no hurry,' Elijah said, and Birdie nodded, taking it all in.

Elijah watched her for a few moments and then turned to Georgina. 'May I have an audience with you later, Miss Urry?' he asked.

'Of course, Doctor, I am at your disposal,' she said and flushed.

Matilda could not help herself and openly studied them with pleasure. After completing his check on Birdie, Elijah rose and, with a nod of goodbye, left the ward. It was then that Matilda's eyes widened as the collection of paintings that were leaning against the wall fell forward. Georgina scrambled to collect them.

'Best tidy these up,' she said before Winifred took them. She studied several, pulled them out and rolling them up, handed them to Matilda.

'We should frame some of these for the ladies,' Matilda said, making an excuse as Winifred approached. 'They are exceptionally good.'

'How thoughtful of you both,' Winifred said.

Thoughtful indeed, Matilda mused with a knowing look towards Georgina. These paintings were going straight to the police station and into the hands of the detectives.

Chapter 28

Thomas entered the chilly rooms of the coroner, Dr Nevins. He waited a moment as the good doctor raised a finger and finished a gruesome task which Thomas could not take his eyes off – the liver slipped into a sterile dish. The smell alone was enough to make Thomas retch; his nose was more sensitive than most. The doctor moved away, washed his hands, and joined him.

'Detective Ashdown!' Dr Nevins looked around him with exaggerated movements. 'No Detective Dart?'

Thomas laughed. 'No, I am not hiding him. He has got a medical appointment this morning, or rather Mrs Dart does, and he is accompanying her. Sorry to interrupt your work in progress.'

'As always?' Dr Nevins said and smiled.

'Yes, well, consistency is to be valued, I believe. I've come to ask about—'

'Yes,' Dr Nevins answered.

'Yes?' Thomas rubbed his hand over his face and breathed out with relief. 'At last, something useful.'

'Laudanum was definitely in Mrs Rodgers' system and given that she was no longer a patient at the asylum, the question is, who administered it to her and why was she taking it?' Dr Nevins asked.

'My thoughts exactly. Thank you, Patrick,' Thomas said and was gone before Dr Nevins had a chance to respond.

Thomas returned to his office, checked his partner was not yet back and reminded himself of the address of Mrs Hilda Rodgers' cousin, Flora Bignell. He left for her abode. Fortunately, she was home. He was well familiar with her street in the less than salubrious neighbourhood that was often a call-out location for break-ins and fights. As before, Flora's home was impeccably kept.

'Detective, you are in luck,' she said, welcoming him in. 'I haven't cleaned out Hilda's rooms or possessions. I couldn't bring myself to do it.'

Thomas nodded and followed her inside. 'I understand.'

'Besides, there is no one waiting to move in. I offered my house to her sons – my nephews – but they seem to enjoy their independence in the rooms above the bakery,' she said, leading the way up the narrow stairs to the room she had given to her cousin to use. She indicated the room.

'May I offer you a cup of tea, Detective?' she asked.

'Thank you, yes, that would be welcome,' Thomas said, feeling thirst and hunger pressing on him. Plus, he wanted Flora Bignall out of the way so he could move around the room without being observed.

He stood in the doorway for a moment and then began the task of opening drawers, looking through clothes and a lady's delicates, which he did most hurriedly before Flora returned, and then searching Hilda Rodgers' small bag of belongings.

'Will you take your tea here?' Flora said, appearing in the doorway with a cup and saucer. 'I can place it on the dresser.'

'Thank you, much appreciated. I shan't delay you for too long,' Thomas said, stopping to take a sip and hungrily appreciating the two home-made biscuits in the saucer. 'Mrs Bignall, your cousin never mentioned she was on any medication, did she?'

Flora shook her head in the negative. 'No, she said she was in pain and as I mentioned last time, Hilda said she intended to see a doctor, but I did not see her taking anything or know of any potions.'

Thomas nodded and returned to the bed. He leaned down to check the bedside drawer and feel under the mattress and pillow. Rising, he saw it, a small medicine bottle that had fallen down the back of the headrest. He picked it up and held it high to see if it still contained any fluid.

Flora gasped. 'That must have been Hilda's. Nobody else has been staying in this room for a very long time.'

Thomas opened the lid and sniffed. The pungent smell of laudanum hit his nostrils.

'Thank you, Mrs Bignall, I have found what I need. I believe this medicine caused your cousin to be confused.'

'Enough to make her take her own life?' Flora asked.

'Very possibly, as she may have been on a euphoric high or experiencing a terrible low. And you definitely have not seen this bottle before or know of who might have provided it to Mrs Rodgers?'

Flora shook her head. 'No. I wish I could help, Detective. I feel a little relieved knowing that a potion might have led her astray, I could not fathom her actions.' She breathed out as if some of the weight on her shoulders had been dislodged. Thomas was sure of her sincerity. 'I won't rest now until you find someone responsible for her death.'

He finished his tea with one quick gulp, and happily taking the leftover biscuit at her suggestion and the medicine bottle, thanked Flora, who saw him out.

'You will let me and the boys know should you discover anything, please?' she asked, standing in the doorway as Detective Ashdown departed.

'Of course,' he said. 'Good morning, Mrs Bignall,' and with that, he continued on his mission.

If Mrs Hilda Rodgers had not yet seen a doctor, and assuming the contact with her husband had been minimal, did someone at the asylum give her the medication before she was signed out? Maybe someone who muttered the word 'criminal' when the last patient didn't succeed in flying. That was where Thomas was heading and exactly what he intended to find out.

⋆⋆⋆⋆⋆

After a quick check back at the station and with no partner still in sight, Thomas made his way to the asylum. He was fired up with the lead, the first real clue he had since Mrs

Hilda Rodgers threw herself from the Victoria Bridge. The bottle found near her murdered husband could belong to the killer, but why was he visiting Mr Rodgers and why kill him?

He barely saw the route on the omnibus as he went through the scenarios and questions in his head. On arrival, he encountered the formidable Matron Marion Gormley, but Thomas had encountered worse.

'Back, Detective?' she asked, stating the obvious.

'You have an excellent memory for faces, Matron,' Thomas said, not intending to flatter her as, unlike his partner, Harry, he did not care for smoothing the way and small talk.

'It won't surprise you that despite the many patients in residence, we don't get many other visitors,' she said with the hint of a smile. 'And who might you be calling on then?'

'I'd like to speak with the doctors, please. Not Dr Hayward, but—'

'Dr O'Shea and Dr McQuade,' she finished for him.

'Yes, Dr McQuade first please if he is in residence,' Thomas said.

'He is; please sign in and then come this way.'

Thomas quickly filled in the required details in the visitor book on the entrance desk and then followed the small, capable director of nursing down the sterile tiled hallway, the sound of their footfalls only interrupted by the occasional scream or yell, each making Thomas flinch. He was not sure why she accompanied him this time, when last time she had allowed himself and Detective Dart to roam.

Maybe it was a new directive in light of the patient who was unaccounted for last week and threatened Matilda, or maybe everyone had to be paired. He didn't care to ask.

The matron led Thomas towards the men's wards where he had visited when the patient had finished his week with falling from a great height, and where he and Harry last visited to try and catch up with Dr O'Shea. He was grateful that Dr O'Shea had been too busy to see them, or he would not have been on hand to rescue Matilda. The thought of his pending proposal brought a smile to his lips.

As they walked, Thomas did his best not to glance in the rooms where he saw movement in his peripheral vision. He saw his share of bad sights and the regular visits to the morgue were plenty enough to keep him topped up without adding fresh material of distressed souls locked in rooms.

The matron stopped suddenly, rapped on a closed door and entered without waiting for an invitation. She announced, 'There's a detective here to see you, Dr McQuade,' and stood aside for Thomas to enter. Thomas thanked her and greeted the doctor. The door was closed behind him and the matron was gone.

'My apologies for the unexpected intrusion,' Thomas said.

The room was large, with a view of the grounds and the gardens where the patients worked. Dr Victor McQuade sat at his desk completing paperwork. He did not rise but stopped what he was doing and indicated a seat to Thomas.

'You're here about the patient who leapt?' he asked,

putting his pen down and giving Thomas his attention. He was a small man with a serious countenance, not yet in his thirtieth year, Thomas estimated.

'Yes, and I am also here about Mrs Hilda Rodgers who leapt from the Victoria Bridge, and Mr Finch Turner, who fell from a great height at the Exhibition Building. We connected all three to the asylum and two of the victims we know had laudanum prescribed to them. What can you tell me of that?' Thomas asked, starting with a broad question to gauge a reaction. He did not mention the bottle found beside the deceased Mr Rodgers.

Dr McQuade drew in a deep breath and sat back, his hands gripping the chair's armrests. He looked outside to the grounds and frowned. 'I have never prescribed that drug myself, ever. It is addictive and the negative effects far outweigh its benefits. But not everyone feels that way.'

Thomas waited. Dr McQuade said nothing further. Frustrated, Thomas tried another angle.

'You were heard to say the word, "criminal" when a female patient tried to jump recently.'

Dr McQuade snapped to look at Thomas, his eyebrows raised in surprise.

'What did you mean by that?' Thomas asked.

'I can't imagine why I would have said that.' He returned his gaze to the garden.

'I think you can,' Thomas said. He could not decide if Dr McQuade was uncomfortable with people or uncomfortable being interrogated, or both. The lack of eye contact made it hard for Thomas to read the doctor.

'Was it criminal that she was stopped or criminal that she had access to the window to leap and was in a state of mind to do so?'

Dr McQuade turned away from the grounds and towards Thomas but looked at the desk as he spoke. 'The medication, the access to the window, the charade that we care, it is all criminal,' he muttered in a low voice that required Thomas to lean forward to hear him. Again, he offered nothing of use.

Thomas pushed Dr McQuade further. 'It is highly plausible that someone from the asylum provided Mrs Hilda Rodgers with the laudanum and encouraged her to take it. Could you suggest who that might be?'

'I could not say, Detective, but it certainly was not me,' Dr McQuade answered, returning his gaze to the garden outside his window. 'It's an interesting drug of choice, though. You could persuade the taker to undertake certain acts – they may be full of bravado and believe they are invincible or they may feel so full of despair that they take the option of release offered to them.'

Thomas's jaw locked with frustration. He was getting nowhere. Who was the supplier, who had access to the male and female patients? Who from the asylum might have visited Mr Raymond Rodgers with a bottle of laudanum in their pocket and why were they carrying it, given Mrs Hilda Rodgers was already dead by then, and it appeared Mr Rodgers was not himself a user? And why were so many other recent 'jumpers' all associated with the asylum being prescribed the same medicine in their systems?

'I haven't as yet checked to see if you have a record with

the police, Dr McQuade. Should I do so?' Thomas asked. 'Is there a reason you are working here if you find the whole thing so *criminal*?'

Dr Mc Quade shook his head in frustration and met Thomas's gaze for the first time. 'You will find no record of me. I work here, Detective, because my mother died in an asylum when I was a boy. I did not understand then what she endured, but I have since learned. On my shift, no patient will endure the indignity of what she suffered.'

'I am sorry,' Thomas said and took a leaf out of his partner's book, remembering to balance his curt interview style with some empathy as required. 'Help me then,' he said, requesting compassion. 'Who is killing these patients and why? Two of them had already been released. How many more are there that we are not aware of yet?'

Before Dr McQuade could answer, the door opened, and Thomas turned to find Dr O'Shea present.

'Ah, the matron said you wanted to speak with the doctors,' he said, smiling. 'I am sorry to interrupt, Detective, Dr McQuade, but I am available now for twenty minutes only, if you wanted to catch me, then I must leave for the day for appointments.'

Thomas rose and thanked Dr McQuade. Frustration boiled up inside him. He was so close to finding out if there was corruption within, and he believed Dr McQuade was intending to help him. But at least he had a reason for not believing Dr McQuade to be suspicious.

He departed with Dr O'Shea and followed him down one hallway and then another, and another, into the bowels of the asylum.

Chapter 29

Thomas's gut instinct – which he honed well in his years of policing – was telling him to turn back now, wait until he had Harry to back him up. But curiosity pulled him forward, and he feared if he did not follow now, he might lose the chance to learn more about the happenings at the asylum. Besides, Dr O'Shea was hardly a threatening figure. The route they were taking, however, was somewhat forbidding.

As if reading his thoughts, Dr O'Shea glanced back and said, 'Not far now.' His face was lit by the lamplight to appear ghostly on one angle, evil on the other.

The hallway was sterile and cold, the smell damp and mildewy, and Thomas could not see what was in any of the rooms off the hallway he traversed, due to the dim light and not having his own lantern in his possession.

'Where exactly are we going and what can I expect to see?' Thomas asked, warily.

'I believe your queries have been concerning the administering of drugs and medication to our patients. Is that correct?' Dr O'Shea asked.

'Yes. While the coroner tells me that deaths are quite common in an asylum, the traces of laudanum on the last three deceased residents or former residents implies they have been administered the drug. Neither Dr McQuade nor Dr Hayward have supplied it.'

'No, that is correct,' Dr O'Shea said. 'There would be little reason for us to prescribe laudanum.' He turned sharply, directly shining the light in Thomas's eyes.

Thomas fell back a step, wincing, blinded, and then he heard hurried footsteps behind him.

'Where have you been?' Dr O'Shea muttered.

'I am sorry, Doctor,' a youthful voice that Thomas could not identify said.

Thomas whirled around, but before he could defend himself, he felt the swift movement of air and a dull hard hit made contact with the back of his head. Fear gripped him as his knees gave out and the floor came up to meet him.

*****

Thomas roused, peacefully at first, as he would do any morning of the week when not chased by nightmares. But that peace was momentary. His eyes shot open, and he attempted to raise his head to determine his location. He could see the thick straps pinning him to the bed. The room was dark, save for one lamp in the corner, and he knew from the smell where he was; in the asylum, unable to move, a prisoner.

His throat was hellishly dry, and he swallowed, panicked.

He strained, testing the binding to no avail, twisting left and right, but he gained no traction.

'Ah, welcome back, Detective,' a voice said, startling him.

Thomas tried to raise his head to see over his shoulder where the voice came from, but winced and dropped back down again. A roaring pain throbbed from his neck to the back of his head. He squinted to find the source of the voice – Dr O'Shea – who then moved beside him.

'As you were so curious about the drug and its effects, I thought I would let you experience it first hand,' Dr O'Shea said, smiling at Thomas. 'There is nothing quite like undertaking your own research, is there?'

A wave of claustrophobia riding on the back of dizziness from the drug hit Thomas. He closed his eyes momentarily as the room closed in, the proximity of Dr O'Shea and his own immobility overwhelmed him. He swallowed down his fear.

'My partner will be looking for me and you can't think you will get away with this,' Thomas said, the effort of speaking irritating his dry throat. He struggled against his bonds.

Dr O'Shea laughed. 'It would amaze you what I have got away with, and this will be no exception, I assure you.'

The doctor, wearing a white jacket and holding a large stethoscope, placed one end on Thomas's chest over the heart, and moved the other end to his ear and listened.

Thomas thrashed.

'Stop moving or I will sedate you immediately,' the doctor snapped without pausing from his listening procedure.

Thomas stilled as best he could and tried to control his breathing. After a minute, which seemed like an hour to Thomas, the doctor pulled away and look down on his patient.

'Hmm, you have had two doses, four hours apart and your breathing is quite short, as expected. Your heart is not racing, but it is certainly accelerated. Therefore, I'll give you another hour until your next dosage.'

'Four hours apart! How long have I been here?' Thomas asked, trying to calculate the time which could not be estimated in the dark room.

'It is quite late,' Dr O'Shea responded but gave no further detail.

Thomas knew his only option was to slow down whatever experiment the doctor intended to do in the hope Harry would find him before it went too far. The irrational fear of being in the dark, restrained in an asylum, left to rot in the damp, was overriding him. It took all his willpower to rise above it.

'I wanted you to be fully awake and lucid between each dosage so we can both enjoy the process,' Dr O'Shea said with a smile. 'The bump was only enough to knock you out so you could be restrained. How are you feeling?' he asked as if Thomas was a patient seeking consultation.

'Is this how you controlled your other patients? You were involved in all of their deaths?' Thomas asked. He wanted a confession and, more so, he wanted time.

'Do you think anyone will miss them?' The doctor made a scoffing sound.

Thomas struggled, his mind thinking of ways he could save himself if it came to that.

'Pulling against your bonds will not work, Detective,' Dr O'Shea informed him in a voice that sounded bored with the process. 'Many have tried before you with no success. They designed the bonds to keep patients restricted, and now you are my patient.'

'Why? Why did you kill them? Was it for a thrill?' Thomas asked.

Dr O'Shea laughed. 'A thrill? No, quite the opposite. It's laborious to manipulate the mind.' He sighed again, as if Thomas were a poor student not grasping his lessons. 'The families pay me very well to end their loved ones' suffering,' he said, admitting his duplicity of pretending to care for his patients while orchestrating their deaths.

Thomas scoffed. 'Their loved ones' suffering? Do you mean their own suffering? Their desire to get their hands on the insurance money or marry again?'

'Can you blame them? Can you imagine having a loved one locked away in here and your life being on hold?'

'Why is their life on hold?' Thomas asked, trying to buy as much time as he could. 'They can go about their business, free of the encumbrance of their ill spouse since they have rendered them incapacitated. And, there is talk of allowing the dissolution of the marriage contract due to insanity.'

'Talk, talk, talk, but no action. But aren't you knowledgeable, Detective? I am impressed.'

Thomas groaned and had to close his eyes again as another

bout of nausea hit him. When the feeling and dizziness passed, he opened his eyes to see the doctor studying him.

'Not pleasant, is it? I can't imagine it is a great life for the families or the patients either,' Dr O'Shea said. 'Consider my actions as saving the patients' loved ones the bother of waiting for death to take their betrothed or going through the indignity of divorce.'

'And profiting nicely,' Thomas said. 'Why did you kill Mr Rodgers? He was not a patient.'

Dr O'Shea moved away to one of the shelves and collected a bottle. He returned to stand over Thomas and look down at him. Thomas pushed as far as he could into the bed, but the leering doctor took pleasure in his helplessness.

'I guess there is no harm in telling you,' Dr O'Shea said. 'You can go to the grave knowing the full story. Will that make you feel better?'

Thomas struggled again, and Dr O'Shea shook his head. 'He wouldn't pay, ungrateful wretch,' he said, his lips thinning in anger.

Thomas stopped. 'Why not?'

'The death was too public for his liking. He wanted Hilda to die while she was at the asylum, but she was too rational. There was not an insane bone in that woman's body but befriend any doctor and they will provide the necessary certificate to make it real,' Dr O'Shea said and shrugged as if it was unfortunate, but of no consequence. He continued, 'I could not get Hilda over the line. I knew she was having some back pain, so I delivered some medication around for her – the laudanum – and told her it would help with her aches.'

'Her cousin said she was intending to see a doctor but did not,' Thomas recalled.

'I told Hilda not to say I had visited as my duty of care was strictly to the asylum, but I had wanted to check on her.'

'How good of you,' Thomas said smartly.

'It did the job, but her husband was an objectionable man and when he refused to pay, then he got what he deserved. Now, Detective, enough time-wasting and confessions. Let's not wait any longer since you are obviously quite lucid. We'll have another dose and another lesson on what the drug can do.' His face lit with pleasure in the control he mastered, and then he momentarily disappeared behind Thomas.

Thomas strained to see the doctor. He fought against his bonds, pure instinct and fear driving him. Stopping, he listened, hearing not a sound anywhere else. Thomas knew better than to call out... the route they took to arrive where he now lay was empty, as cold as a tomb. He did not want to lie here unconscious and unprotected for hours on end.

His body arched with fear as Dr O'Shea approached him. The doctor held a hypodermic syringe and, ignoring Thomas's futile struggle, put it straight through the detective's shirt and emptied the contents into Thomas's arm, then stood back to watch the reaction on his patient's face. Thomas's features eased; his body relaxed.

'Now doesn't that feel good?' Dr O'Shea said. 'Soon you will enjoy the euphoric feeling that comes with it. I will return after a few hours, and I will watch you come down. We can share that experience too.'

Thomas struggled against it, but the fight was futile. He

felt as if he was floating, that the stress had left his body. He was walking on air.

'It will make you feel as if you can fly,' Dr O'Shea said with a smile.

Chapter 30

It was just before tea time when a knock at the Hayward front door summoned Harriet as she was about to retire from her duties for the evening. Detective Dart stood on the doorstep on the chilly evening, hoping for answers. Harriet opened the door and greeted him.

'Detective Dart, always a pleasure,' she said and smiled.

'Good evening, Harriet.' He removed his hat and before he could say another word, Matilda bounded from the dining room on hearing the doorbell and Harriet's address of 'Detective'.

'Detective Dart!' Matilda exclaimed and then she stopped dead in her tracks, her face fell, and her legs felt weak. 'Oh no, you have come to tell me bad news.' Her hand went to her heart and Matilda's face went a shade of white. Mr Hayward and Miss Georgina Urry appeared beside her.

'No, that is not the case, I assure you. Do not concern yourself please, Miss Hayward, Mr Hayward, Miss Urry.' Detective Dart held up his hand.

'But you are seeking Thomas, are you not?' Matilda asked. 'He is not here. I've invited Georgina to dinner. I wasn't expecting Thomas tonight.'

'Understandable. I have been out of the office a good half of the day and our paths did not cross, that is all,' he assured them. 'Please do not fret.'

Harry could tell Matilda was not convinced. The small party came towards him. Georgina came to Matilda's side, linking arms with her in support.

Harry continued, 'Is he out with Daniel, perhaps?'

'No,' Matilda responded firmly. 'Daniel has gone to the ballet with Alice. But you have had no success locating him at your work and you have gone to his home, have you not? Was Teddy there?' she asked.

'Well, yes. Teddy says he is not home yet, but he is expecting him soon,' Harry said, but he could not mask the anxiety on his face.

'We need to show the detective,' Georgina said, and Matilda nodded.

'Show me what?' Harry asked and Matilda departed momentarily.

'I imagine you have tried his usual pub haunts too, Detective Dart?' Mr Hayward asked.

Harry nodded. 'I have, and he was not there. His colleagues in attendance had not seen him. It may be nothing.'

Georgina explained to the detective, Mr Hayward, and Harriet who stood by the door, 'We found some very telling drawings from the lady residents of the asylum,' she said. 'We brought them home with us today and were going to deliver them to you and Detective Ashdown in the morning, Detective Dart.'

Matilda returned with the scrolls. She unrolled them and displayed several paintings that patients had done of themselves in flight, with wings, or standing on high perches ready to leap into the air.

'Good grief,' Mr Hayward said.

'Considering how many deaths we have had recently, this is most concerning,' Harry said, agreeing with their assumptions.

'He has gone to the asylum, I am sure of it,' Matilda said.

'I fear you are right,' Harry said. 'He intended to speak with the doctor you overheard the other day and with the head doctor.' Harry did not mention the laudanum or that the coroner had advised that Thomas came by and was informed that laudanum was found in Mrs Rodgers' body. Harry suspected Thomas most likely left to investigate if an asylum doctor in residence had administered it.

'Let us go then,' Matilda said.

'No! Absolutely not,' Harry said in a firmer voice than he usually used. 'It is far too dangerous, Miss Hayward, I must insist.'

He heard Mr Hayward sigh as if he was fighting a losing battle.

Matilda continued. 'Elijah is out with Gideon. I know where they are. Georgina and I will show you and wait in the carriage while you fetch him. You will need him at the asylum; he will gain us entry.'

Harry had to concede that was the way forward, and he had no intention of leaving Thomas missing for the evening.

'I shall find him if you tell me where Elijah is this evening,' Harry responded.

'We can do more together, please Detective Dart,' Matilda said. 'Georgina, you need not come of course.'

'I shall indeed,' she insisted.

'With your permission, Mr Hayward?' Harry asked, surrendering.

Mr Hayward nodded. 'I suspect Matilda will go with or without you, Detective, so I'd prefer she was in your company.'

'Thank you,' Harry said, pleased for the support. 'Let us make haste.'

*****

Elijah looked surprised to see Detective Harry Dart approaching him and Gideon. He leapt to his feet.

'What is it, Harry?' he asked, his face a mask of concern.

'I need you to come to the asylum with me, Elijah. Will you, right this minute? I'll explain on the way,' Harry said.

'Of course,' he said, excusing himself from Gideon, who offered to come but was told it was best he stayed or headed home.

It surprised Elijah to see his sister and Miss Urry waiting outside in a hansom. Matilda hurried down, unassisted.

'Matilda! Miss Urry! What on earth is the matter?' Elijah hastened to them, nodding his head in a small, courteous bow to Miss Urry.

'We will tell you on the way, Elijah. Please hurry. I will

travel with you, Detective Dart, if that is suitable? Georgina can get Elijah up to speed,' Matilda said and within moments they were in the two hansoms, making haste to the asylum.

Elijah took a shaky breath. He had undertaken operations, passed medical examinations and endured the harshest scrutiny from his instructors, but it was Miss Urry sitting so visibly close to him that set his heart racing.

'I hoped to call on you, Miss Urry, but not quite like this,' Elijah said kindly as he settled beside her.

'Do not worry, Dr Hayward, my life is rarely conventional,' she said with a small chuckle.

'Elijah, please,' he insisted but mindful of not taking liberties as they sat together, alone, and with the urgency at hand, he cleared his throat and said, 'Forgive me for being direct, please tell me what is going on?'

'Of course,' she said, her cheeks flushed, and had Elijah been able to see her heart, he would have seen it had swelled in his company.

She recounted what had unfolded.

He studied Georgina as she told him in a frank and welcome manner the source of the distress. Elijah rubbed a hand over his face.

'Thomas should never have gone there alone,' he said. 'There is something afoot, but I have not been there long enough to discover what.'

'We found some patients' drawings,' she said, quickly explaining the flying theme to him.

The hansoms turned into the grounds and made their way to the entrance.

Elijah turned to Georgina. 'I know you are a very sensible and capable woman, Georgina,' he said, using her name for the first time and enjoying the sound of it on his tongue. She smiled on hearing his familiarity. 'But this could be dangerous. We do not know what to expect. Please be cautious for your sake, and as a personal favour to me, please try to manage Matilda as best you can.'

She nodded, and within moments, Elijah had alighted. He quickly offered his hand to Georgina, who did not delay him with a genteel or flirtatious exit, but alighted speedily, despite the fluttering feeling that overwhelmed her at the touch of his hand. They entered.

The asylum looked sinister in the light of day; at night, it appeared frightening at best, evil at worst. Howls, yells and noise could be heard coming from various wards.

'I thought it would be quiet and that our arrival would be invasive,' Matilda said, hurrying up the stairs behind the detective and her brother.

'The night brings out more anxieties than the day for those who do not sleep,' Elijah said.

They entered and found Dr McQuade on duty. It was his week for the evening shift. His eyes widened at seeing the small party.

'Elijah… Dr Hayward!' he said formalising his address on seeing Elijah in the company of others. 'What is going on?' he asked, stopping by the matron's reception desk.

'This is Detective Dart, and you have met Miss Hayward and Miss Urry. We are seeking Detective Ashdown, have you seen him?' Elijah asked hurriedly.

'Yes.'

Elijah heard Matilda's breath hitch.

'But many hours ago,' Dr McQuade said. 'He came to speak with me about the use of laudanum and the administration of it.'

'About what hour was this, Dr McQuade?' Harry asked, staying calm.

'Very early afternoon, not long past midday. But he had to leave as Dr O'Shea arrived and could only see him then or not at all. He cut our interview short and followed him,' Dr McQuade said.

'I don't think he left,' Elijah said.

Dr McQuade stood to full height and grabbed a lantern. 'Come with me.'

Before they had progressed more than a few steps, Dr McQuade had other ideas. He stopped, bringing the party to a halt, and addressed Elijah.

'I'm sorry, Dr Hayward, but I think it is best if the ladies stay here,' Dr McQuade said.

'Why?' Matilda asked impatiently, her voice laced with emotion. Georgina took her hand, and Elijah gave her a grateful look. Initially, he was frustrated to see both ladies in attendance, especially knowing Georgina would not have come without Matilda insisting on being present. Now he was grateful Georgina was there.

'I'm sorry, but I can't allow you to come. I am in charge of this hospital this evening, and that is how it is,' he said firmly, holding Matilda's gaze. 'For your safety, madam,' he added.

Not wishing to hold them up from the mission despite wanting to attend, Matilda turned to Elijah and Detective Dart. 'Please hurry.'

Elijah took her free hand. 'Do not fret, we will do our

best.' He glanced at Georgina, the sight of her lighting a passion in his chest and turned to follow Dr McQuade with Detective Dart by his side.

'Where are you taking us, Victor?' Elijah asked addressing him informally now it was just the three of them and they had recently become acquainted on a first-name basis.

'There are rooms away from the general precinct where I believe Dr O'Shea has set himself up to do… experiments.' He chose his words diplomatically.

Harry muttered, 'For the love of God.'

Elijah saw his stressed expression. Thomas was his protégé and close friend. Harry loved him like a son.

They hurried on.

'How did you discover this?' Elijah asked.

'I didn't,' Dr McQuade said and explained, 'I have only suspected it.' He glanced at Detective Dart as he hurried them down another corridor, through the maze of the asylum wards. The small light thrown from his lamp cast eerie shadows on the walls.

Elijah hoped all patients were accounted for and in their beds. A random attack would not be welcome.

Dr McQuade continued. 'I have only been working here six months and have noticed behaviour from my patients that was inconsistent with their treatments. I suspected Dr O'Shea was dosing patients for his own gain, and so I have been doing my own subtle investigation for a few months. I've had to be careful.'

'No doubt,' Harry said in agreement.

'I was just about to broach my findings with Detective

Ashdown when we were interrupted,' Dr McQuade said. 'But there are things I can share with you, Detective, should your investigations necessitate it – excessive deaths for one.'

'Thank you, Dr McQuade. Your findings would be of great interest,' Harry said and then Dr McQuade slowed down as they came to a set of stairs leading to a lower level and warned them to keep quiet.

'I don't know if Dr O'Shea, your detective, or anyone is down here,' he said in a hushed voice, 'but let us be cautious.'

Elijah and Harry nodded. Elijah hoped Dr McQuade was trustworthy and not in cahoots with Dr O'Shea and leading them astray. He wondered what the hell he had got himself into and knew if he didn't come back with his future brother-in-law in one piece, he would break his sister's heart, not to mention his big brother, Daniel's, who had been Thomas's best friend since childhood. He tried to calm himself, which he had told his patients to do when the occasion called for it. Not an easy task. He would learn from this experience.

They wandered down a dark hallway, following the flickering lamp held by Dr McQuade. Elijah prayed it would not be extinguished. They were so low in the bowels of the central building that Elijah did not know that these rooms existed. Harry turned to him and even in the shadows, Elijah understood the look that Harry gave him – not to trust anyone. He nodded and took comfort in the fact that Harry, despite his years, was a champion boxer in his day and could still throw a punch or two with impact if needed.

Dr McQuade held up a lamp to each room, gazing through the small inspection window. They were all empty.

Except for one.

Dr McQuade nodded towards the room and stood slightly to the side, allowing the light to shine through and Elijah and Harry to see.

'Goodness!' Harry exclaimed. 'Is that a laboratory?'

'Of sorts,' Dr McQuade said and opened the door.

'There must be hundreds of pounds worth of medicine here,' Elijah said in awe, looking around but not leaving the entrance way for fear of being locked in. After all, they could not be sure that Dr Victor McQuade was on their side.

'A huge stock,' Dr McQuade agreed. 'I discovered it a couple of months ago. I don't know who knows it is here, but to think we struggle to get medication.' He shook his head and then looked uncomfortable.

'What is it?' Elijah asked.

'I have not gone any further into the building, as I was fearful of what might happen if I were caught out alone. But I have heard screams and yells,' he said with a nod to the darkened hallway in front of them.

'Then let's make haste,' Harry said. 'We have no time to waste.'

Chapter 32

'Waiting is terrible,' Georgina said as she paced up and down the reception area. Now and then a scream or wail affronted the two ladies.

'I have no intention of waiting,' Matilda assured her, anxious in the unoccupied suspense of allowing the men to move from sight. 'I am just leaving it long enough for the men to get ahead so we can begin our own investigation.'

Georgina straightened up. 'Well, you are full of surprises. That is something I would do, but I thought you might be more tender of heart.'

Matilda smiled despite her distress. 'With four brothers, I think that was buffed out of me many years ago.' She snapped to look at an orderly walking out of a room up the hallway but about to go in the other direction.

'Mr Derichs,' she called, not fearful of waking anyone up, as there was noise aplenty. She saw his eyes widen, and he turned and hurried towards her, a look of confusion on his countenance.

'Miss Hayward,' he said and gave a small bow.

'Please may I introduce Miss Georgina Urry,' Matilda said, speaking fast.

'Nikolaus Derichs at your service, Miss Urry,' he said formerly. 'What are you both doing here at this hour?'

Georgina stepped in. 'Matilda's beau is missing and was last seen here – Detective Thomas Ashdown. We came here with Detective Dart, but he went that way,' she said, pointing down the hallway, 'accompanied by Dr McQuade and Dr Hayward, and Dr McQuade instructed us to remain here.'

Nikolaus Derichs's face fell at the mention of a beau for Matilda, but he cleared his throat and offered his services.

'I will not wait, I'm sorry, Mr Derichs,' Matilda said. 'I hope you will not try to stop us too. Could you help us?'

'What can I do to assist?' he asked, and Matilda exhaled with relief.

'Thank you. Where do you place your most troublesome patients when you want them out of the way and not seen or heard from? Where might Detective Ashdown be held if he were captive?' she asked.

He nodded. 'I shall get a lamp. Come with me if you do not fear dark places?'

'We are right behind you,' Georgina assured him and, arm in arm, the ladies followed in close pursuit.

Matilda had never been so grateful for the support of a woman, a sister that she never had, with Georgina by her side.

*****

The three men continued down the blackened hallway, lit only by the one small lamp Dr McQuade carried in front. They stopped long enough to look into each room as they encountered it. Each room looked prepared and ready for a patient, but the wing was ghostly empty.

'Why are these rooms not used?' Harry asked, his voice subdued, but echoing along the hallway. 'I thought the asylum was overcrowded and seeking funding.'

'Damp, I believe,' Dr McQuade said and sniffed the air.

'That is most likely the reason,' Elijah said, agreeing with him. 'We are very close to the river here and I understand that parts of the building flooded last time there was a deluge.'

The men could smell the damp as if it is presented itself on cue.

Harry uncharacteristically swore under his breath. 'He must be somewhere. I am tempted to call out his name.'

'Patience, just a little longer,' Dr McQuade asked of the detective. 'Let us finish this wing first, in case we are not alone. Once we've exhausted the search of the remaining rooms, we can resort to that. Yes?'

Harry agreed. 'I shall give him what-for when we find him for coming here alone.'

Harry's positive thinking comforted Elijah… they had to find Thomas and find him alive. He was terrified that Thomas had been drugged and was not below in the lower wings but somewhere high, preparing to fall from some great height with no one to see who might be assisting his fall.

The men hurried, studying each area as best they could to ensure Thomas was not lying prone or trapped inside the cell. It was then that they heard a yell behind them.

'What was that?' Elijah asked, startled.

'This way,' Dr McQuade said, and all three turned and raced back down the hallway to where the loud voice had come, Dr McQuade leading the way with his light bouncing off the walls and floor, and Elijah and Harry in close pursuit.

*****

Nikolaus Derichs glanced back at the two women following him with blind faith. 'Some of the other orderlies and I come down here when we want a break from the madness,' he said, hurriedly leading Matilda and Georgina whom he found most capable and requiring no assistance.

'How awful,' Georgina said. 'Why would you not seek sunshine and fresh air?'

'Because here no one sees us, should we wish to smoke or… if the boys wish to meet with a nurse,' he said, attempting delicacy.

Matilda grimaced, not that anyone could see her expression. 'I would be scared that I would be locked in here,' she said. 'Do you think Thomas is down here, somewhere?'

'There are several rooms that Dr O'Shea told us to bring patients for him. They are set up for treatment, but away from the main hospital,' Nikolaus said.

'Why would Dr O'Shea want to treat patients away from the main hospital?' Georgina asked, 'unless he was doing something not lawful, perhaps.'

'I cannot say,' Nikolaus said. 'All I know is it is very hard to hear noises from down here and very private, and Dr O'Shea says his work is important for the medical fraternity and future health of all patients.'

'I bet he does,' Matilda said, less than impressed. She hurried to keep up as both Nikolaus and Georgina were a good head taller than herself, with longer legs and extended strides. Matilda felt nauseous at the thought of Thomas being experimented on and did her best not to dwell on it… not to think about how many hours Thomas had been in the asylum and what might have happened between the time he met with Dr O'Shea this afternoon and now, but her mind kept playing the thought back over and over.

A sound nearby made Matilda stop. She turned, her body alert. She could feel someone nearby, watching. Matilda's heart raced and when she turned the light was out of sight and Nikolaus and Georgina were well ahead. The spill of the lamp faded to black. She hurried along in the dark, holding her skirts, feeling her terror rising, swearing she could feel someone or something breathing nearby. Her heart was pounding.

She heard Georgina's voice nearby, calling her name.

'I am coming,' Matilda called back and rounded the corner. They were in sight, stopped, waiting for her. The moment of terror had passed, but her heart rate did not slow. Was this what Thomas was going through? Was he imprisoned somewhere down here?

'I thought we had lost you,' Georgina said, alarmed.

'There was a noise, nearby. I stopped and then lost sight of the lamp,' Matilda said.

'It is as though the walls breathe down here,' Nikolaus said, sympathising with her reaction. 'I am sure I have felt someone watching me and nearby me when I have walked these corridors.' He raced down four stairs holding the lamp so the ladies could see them, and advanced when they were in the clear. A few steps after, he stopped abruptly.

'In here,' he said, and the ladies pulled up short to avoid running into him. He opened a door and held up the lamp.

The thought flashed through Matilda's mind that this could be a trap. She was foolish to follow him so blindly and to lead Georgina into danger. It was too late now, too late to turn around and they would never find their way back in the dark, and then Georgina gasped, and Matilda rushed to her side to see for herself the source of her shock.

In the centre of the room, strapped to a bed and lying perfectly still, as if dead, was Detective Thomas Ashdown.

Matilda yelled his name in fright.

Chapter 33

'It came from down there,' Harry said and ran towards a dim light that was brighter only because of the dark surroundings in the long hallway. In the distance, he could see a room with a door ajar.

'Be careful,' Dr McQuade said, keeping alongside the detective as best he could. 'Someone might be in there with your detective.'

Harry did not care. He ran towards the light and straight into the room, Elijah on his coattails and Dr McQuade right behind. His eyes widened at seeing the ladies had got there before him. And then, seeing Thomas lying in the supine position, strapped down on the table; he rushed to his side.

'Miss Hayward, Miss Urry, please step out,' he said, remembering his duty, as he felt Thomas's neck. He scanned for a pulse and, on finding it, exhaled.

Elijah was at Thomas's side in moments, lifting his eyelids and trying to determine Thomas's state of health.

Harry saw Matilda's eyes were wide, her face pale. She grasped Thomas's hand, as if she expected him to wake at any moment and willing it would make it so. The sight of his form lying as if life had left him frightened her so that at first, she could not speak. She blinked and stared as if her heart would stop beating.

'He is alive,' Harry told her and saw her close her eyes and draw a breath. 'Who is this then?' Harry studied the orderly while Georgina worked on loosening the ties around Thomas's arms and feet. Nikolaus assisted.

'He helped us,' Georgina spoke up and added, for Dr McQuade's benefit, 'We would have gone alone, but he would not allow it.'

Nikolaus gave her a grateful look and introduced himself to the detective.

Dr McQuade said, 'There will be time for questions later; we must tend to the detective.'

'He would not want you to see him like this, Miss Hayward,' Harry said, trying to move her back.

'But I must see him, Detective Dart, when he needs me. It is my duty,' she said.

Harry studied her. 'I cannot argue with that, Miss Hayward, but I need to preserve the scene and I know he will want his dignity.'

'And we need to have some room to work,' Dr McQuade said curtly. 'Please just step back and allow us a moment for Detective Ashdown's health.'

Harry took over the role of unstrapping Thomas as Matilda, Georgina, and Nikolaus moved to the doorway.

Thomas stirred as the two doctors tended him. His eyes focused on Dr McQuade and then Elijah.

'I am not dead if you are not the coroner,' he mumbled.

Elijah chuckled. 'No, rest assured, Thom, you are in no need of Dr Nevins.'

Harry waited impatiently as Elijah studied Thomas.

'Laudanum,' Elijah said in a low voice, smelling it on Thomas's breath.

Dr McQuade agreed with Elijah's diagnosis.

Thomas lifted his head and looked at the surrounding party. His eyes found Matilda and widened. He said her name.

She rushed to him, took his hand, kissing it, as tears welled in her eyes.

Elijah touched her shoulder in support.

'You will be well again, Thomas, fear not,' she said, hopeful that the prognosis which she had not yet heard from her brother would concur.

'You will be fine,' Elijah assured Thomas and his sister.

Thomas struggled for control. His eyes closed then reopened, and he looked surprised as if seeing everyone for the first time.

'Harry,' Thomas muttered, noticing him. 'Please don't let Matilda see me like this.'

'But I am here, Thomas,' she said, squeezing his hand, and he turned his head slowly to see her.

'Matilda. Are we married yet?'

Matilda smiled; her eyes filled with tears. 'No. Not yet.'

'Are you sure? Because I am sure we are. I was there.' Thomas frowned, slurring his words. 'You were there too, Elijah and Harry.'

'We will all be there when the time comes,' Matilda assured him, holding his hand.

He closed his eyes again, fading away as the doctors continued their checks. Then suddenly, Thomas's eyes opened. He pulled his hand from Matilda's and struck out, narrowly missing Dr McQuade, as he struggled to get up. Harry hurried forward and restrained him and on seeing Harry's face, Thomas calmed, his eyes roaming across the faces present.

'Matilda, you should not be here,' he said on seeing her.

'I told Miss Hayward that you would not want her to see you like this,' Harry offered, as the doctors brought Thomas to a sitting position. 'But Miss Hayward knows her mind,' he said with a smile in her direction.

She gave Detective Dart a grateful smile. 'We need to get you to a hospital,' she said, returning her attention to Thomas.

'No,' Thomas said firmly. 'No, Elijah.' He turned to his future brother-in-law.

'Thom, calm yourself,' Elijah said.

Thomas looked at the orderly and frowned; Harry followed his gaze to Nikolaus Derichs before Thomas's head dropped back and the doctors laid him on the bed.

He closed his eyes and frowned at the aching of his head. 'I am going to be sick,' Thomas muttered.

'Matilda, please,' Elijah insisted. 'Everyone out except Dr McQuade and Detective Dart,' and with Thomas alive and in good hands, the rest of the party agreed, moving out of the room as Thomas retched, gripped in the caring hands of his future brother-in-law and his mentor.

Chapter 34

Matilda did not expect to sleep well, but yet she woke surprised to have done so. Knowing her brother, Elijah, had spent the night at Thomas's side should he need medical assistance, had provided much relief. Yet again, she was grateful for his calm and caring countenance. She had profusely thanked Georgina for being by her side. The risk her friend had taken would never be forgotten. After dressing and performing her morning toilet, she hurried downstairs. It was a workday and there was a story to tell.

'Good morning, Harriet,' she said, greeting the dutiful house manager before sticking her head into the kitchen to greet Cook. It was a small and informal household that had grown and bent together through many a storm, including the death of Matilda's mother. She entered the dining room to find her father already in attendance reading his half of the paper – the other half waiting for her in her place setting.

'Is there anything in the paper yet, Pa, about the asylum murders?'

'Not as yet,' her father assured her, 'but I suspect you will change that,' he added and smiled at her with affection.

'We are on deadline, and if Thomas will tell me what happened and allow me to run with it, Mrs Lawson may break the story first. Well, the early part of it, anyway. How exciting.'

Mr Hayward agreed as Matilda selected a slice of toast at the sideboard and spooned some butter and jam on her plate, not wishing to spend too long at breakfast.

Her father added: 'He's a very lucky young man. It could have ended much worse.'

Matilda nodded as she took her seat. 'I have never been more terrified, Pa,' she said. 'When I saw Thomas lying there tied up on that bed, my heart stopped. I couldn't imagine my life without Thomas. I can't remember when he wasn't in our lives.'

'Well, I can, but I've got a head start on you,' Mr Hayward said, teasing her, and she gave him an affectionate smile.

Matilda and her father ate in silence for a little while, reading their sections of the paper. As they exchanged newspaper extracts, Matilda asked, 'Do tell me your thoughts upon Georgina.'

He smiled. 'Despite our interrupted dinner, from the time I had with Miss Urry, I found her to be a refreshing and sensible young woman. I've always had a soft spot for a person who calls a spade a spade.'

'I suspect that comes from her life on the farm, and in your case, from years of practising law. But she is wonderful, isn't she? I am sure Elijah is quite taken by her. A surprising choice for him,' Matilda mused.

'Yes and no,' Mr Hayward said. 'He was always a reserved child and happy to be in Gideon's shadow. I think he would be very comfortable with a practical woman who would rather tend to home and business than attend the ballet and theatre. I could see him happily ensconced in a country practice. Country doctors are the heart of the community, and he has a big heart.'

'He has,' she agreed and smiled, thinking of him now tending her beloved Thomas. 'At least if Elijah and Georgina should plan a future together, he will not be too far from home if they move to Georgina's family's region,' Matilda added.

'We are definitely getting more ladies around our table. It has not gone unnoticed that several of them are your doing, dear.'

Matilda laughed. 'Fortunate for me, but not intentional.'

'Well, I am delighted with them all – Minnie, Alice, Georgina should that relationship eventuate, and I am yet to meet Miss Lily Chappell,' Mr Hayward said. 'But I will only have one son-in-law, and I am very happy with your choice when you make it official,' he said with a wink.

*****

Thomas could hear Elijah and his nephew, Teddy, talking in the kitchen as he finished his grooming in his bedroom. It had been a fitful night. He had not felt his best, and the constant checking from Teddy, and Elijah – who had kindly slept on the couch to monitor him – had exasperated him.

Thomas did not return to Matilda's home despite the many bedrooms and willingness of her for him to do so. He did not want her to see him like this, and Harry understood well enough to prevent it. Now, he felt worse for knowing that Elijah and Teddy would suffer for lack of sleep today, too.

Thomas left his room to join them just as the front door swung open and Daniel walked in.

'You're alive!' Daniel proclaimed, removing his hat and giving his best friend a hard slap on the back in an awkward embrace. 'I am pleased for it.'

'As am I,' Thomas agreed with a smile.

'Still, you do not look well.' Daniel studied his friend's pale countenance. 'I wanted to come last night, but Matilda thought I'd best leave you in Elijah's hands,' he said, following Thomas into the kitchen where Teddy had prepared breakfast and Elijah kept him company.

'Just in time,' Teddy greeted Daniel as he filled three plates with eggs, bacon and toast, and one plate with dry toast.

'I hoped as much.' Daniel grinned. 'Although my priority was checking on Thom, of course.'

Thomas scoffed. He knew his friend all too well.

'So how is he, doc?' Daniel asked his younger brother about his best friend's condition.

Elijah looked at Thomas. 'Well, the *patient* was lucky that he only had three doses administered to him, so there will be no long-term effects, but he should be in bed for another day.'

Thomas smirked. 'Thanks, doc.'

The Hayward men, along with Thomas and Teddy, took their seats.

'You are welcome to eggs and bacon,' Teddy said to his uncle, noting his reaction did not welcome the suggestion, 'but the good doctor said dry toast might be all you can stomach.'

Thomas nodded and looked at the plate of toast in front of him. He pushed it slightly away. He ran his tongue over his dry lips.

'No offence, Teddy,' he said and took a deep breath.

Elijah continued. 'The *patient* may also feel slightly depressed, nauseous, have no appetite and experience a dry mouth.'

All eyes turned to Thomas, and he nodded, then cleared his throat to address his friends and nephew.

'I am sorry about last night,' he said. 'Sorry if I struck out at you, Elijah and Teddy, and for keeping you awake all night.'

'Sounds like one of our nights' out,' Daniel joked, breaking the tension, and Thomas gave him a thankful smile.

'It's no problem, Uncle,' Teddy assured him, 'anytime. Well, not too often, you've got a reasonable right hook.'

Elijah nodded. 'I'm just glad you are okay. I couldn't imagine having to tell Matilda or Daniel… well, you know. But please do not exert yourself today.'

Thomas nodded. He turned to Daniel. 'Is Matilda all right this morning?' he asked. 'She has not decided that she can't live with a policeman's life?' His heart stopped beating while he waited for Daniel's assurances, but Teddy spoke first.

'It cannot be easy to be the loved one of those whose work puts them in danger. There are limits to all of our powers of endurance,' he agreed.

Thomas turned to Daniel, his face not masking his anxiety; Daniel could read him and did not jest.

'Not at all, don't be concerned, Thom. Quite the contrary,' Daniel said.

Thomas exhaled again and Elijah smiled at him. It was still a little odd for the Hayward brothers to see their childhood companion, Thomas, and their sister, Matilda, romantically involved after all the years of growing up together.

Daniel continued, 'Be warned, however. She intends to raid your offices this morning and demand an interview and to run the story first, I believe. Good luck with that.'

Thomas groaned, and the men laughed around the table.

'She's unique, your beautiful sister,' Teddy said, addressing the Hayward brothers. He did not admit that Matilda enthralled him from the first time he met her, coming to her rescue at the Freak Show. He saw the look Thomas gave him and added, 'Best you snap her up, Uncle, or someone else will.'

'You?' Thomas asked.

Teddy smiled. 'I am not good enough for Miss Hayward. She can aspire higher than a prison chef.'

'I don't know, Teddy, if you cook up a storm, you could win her over,' Daniel said, and then turned to see the look Thomas was giving him and laughed.

'Ah, Thom, I am sorry. We should not tease you today when you are not in the best condition. We'll save it until you feel better.'

Thomas rolled his eyes at his friend. He sat back, feeling the worse for wear, and felt Daniel's hand on his shoulder. 'Something to look forward to then,' Thomas muttered.

Chapter 35

'Ah, Detective Ashdown – so your partner found you, then?' John, the desk sergeant said, greeting Thomas as he entered.

'He did. Thank you, John. Speaking of which, is Harry in yet?' Thomas asked, hoping he wasn't. He wanted to get his head straight before making the next round of apologies and to sit and regain his strength.

'No, the coast is clear,' John said with a grin. Word had travelled fast by the sound of it. Thomas was not looking forward to Harry's arrival. Harry gave his young protégé considerable freedom and few ties, but Thomas suspected he had snapped them well and truly this time. Despite Elijah's protests that he should rest, Thomas arrived early to study the board and prepare for the arrest they would make today, if they could find Dr Stephen O'Shea, and make no mistake, Thomas intended to find him.

Twenty minutes later, he heard him before he saw him – a familiar footfall. Harry glanced into Thomas's office and sighed on seeing him. He entered.

'You should at least take a day or so to recover. Did not Elijah advise it?' Harry asked of his young partner as he removed his coat and hat, throwing them over a spare chair by Thomas's desk. 'I can't imagine how you got past the good doctor.'

'It wasn't easy.' Thomas had the good grace to look sheepish. He led on the front foot. 'I am sorry, Harry,' he started. 'I returned to the station several times but as you were not back, I did not think I would be in any danger seeing two doctors in a crowded asylum.'

'No?' Harry asked. 'Not at any point?'

Thomas averted his eyes and gave a small shrug. 'Well, when Dr O'Shea suggested I follow him and we kept getting deeper into the unused wing of the hospital asylum, I felt uneasy. But I thought he was a slight man; I could take him.'

Harry indicated a chair and the two men sat. Thomas knew Harry would have to report to the establishment, and it was his duty to cooperate as best he could.

'Did you sleep?' Harry asked.

Thomas shook his head. 'It is the strangest of drugs,' he said as if fascinated to have been part of the experiment. 'I was so weary and numb as if I could sleep for a year, yet I could not get comfortable no matter how I lay.'

Harry nodded. 'Interesting when you apply that to our victims.'

'Indeed,' Thomas agreed. 'Dr O'Shea had only exposed me for a day with several very large doses, but long-term exposure would take its toll. All night, I tossed and turned and could not stay in one position for longer than a few minutes.'

'Poor Teddy and Elijah, we should have taken you to the hospital,' Harry said in retrospect.

'I had some apologising to do this morning,' Thomas agreed. 'I was so irritable last night that I bit their head off each time they came near me, and at once stage I was very disorientated and struck them, thinking I was being attacked.'

'Teddy is big enough to handle you,' Harry said.

Thomas nodded his agreement and closed his eyes momentarily until a feeling of dizziness passed. When he opened them, he swallowed and said, 'I confess, at one stage I felt quite suicidal myself.'

Harry's eyes widened, but Thomas held up his hands.

'Do not concern yourself. At that point I was lucid enough to know why the feelings were coming and going, but had I been Mrs Rodgers, Mr Turner, or any of the other poor recipients, well, I can understand them giving into the feeling.'

'For the love of God,' Harry muttered and shook his head.

Thomas continued. 'I am sorry that you will have to answer for my actions.' He ran his tongue over his lower lip, uncomfortable with the discussion and still dehydrated.

'Son, I don't care about that. I've been in trouble many times over the years, especially when I was a lad your age and starting in the police force. I was a little too handy with my fists on many occasions.'

Thomas couldn't imagine it given the peacekeeper Harry was today.

'What concerns me, is that you could have been

murdered.' Harry's voice rose with a hint of anger. 'Imagine how we would all have to carry on after that.'

Thomas nodded, aware of the consequences of his actions.

Harry drew the picture for him. 'Miss Hayward would be devastated having to bury you, Daniel and Teddy would be at a loss, and I am far too old to break in a new partner – I would have to retire earlier than planned,' he said with a small grin his partner's way.

Thomas smiled. 'It won't happen again.'

'Of course it will,' Harry conceded, 'but with luck, I'll beat it out of you before I hand in my badge and hang up my gloves. We would have found you eventually, before it was not too late I hope, but I take my hat off to Miss Hayward, Miss Urry and the young orderly for discovering you first.'

'Matilda has a nose for drama,' Thomas said with a smile. 'Still, if it had not been for her insights – the paintings, helping Elijah to find the medicine bottle administered to the dressmaker who tried to jump, and sharing the opinions of those who knew Mrs Rodgers to be sane, it might have taken longer to connect it all.'

The two men thought on that for a moment and then Harry asked, 'So, what happened?'

'That's what we would like to know,' a female voice said, and both detectives turned to find John, the desk sergeant, in the doorway with Matilda and Georgina.

'Forgive the interruption, Detective Dart,' Matilda said and thanked the desk sergeant for escorting them.

'Not at all ladies, a pleasant surprise. Please, come in,' Harry said, rising, and clearing two chairs for both ladies.

'Matilda, Miss Urry.' Thomas got to his feet, not quite as steadily.

Matilda played the game she had started earlier with Thomas and introduced them both to the amusement of the group. 'Miss Matilda Hayward and Miss Georgina Urry of the *Women's Journal* requesting an interview please, detectives,' she said.

Thomas moved to Matilda, his smile wide, and taking her hand, kissed it. He welcomed Georgina. 'I am sorry ladies, about last night, the state you found me in.'

'It could not be helped Detective, I am sure, or else you would not be there in the first instance,' Georgina said, ever practical. Harry chuckled.

'That is true, Miss Urry, thank you,' Thomas said. 'Nevertheless, the last thing I want to do is cause distress,' he said, studying his beloved's face.

'Should you put me through that again, Thomas, I may have to dispose of you myself,' Matilda said, most decidedly.

'There are so many inventive ways these days,' Georgina agreed. 'I am sure I've learned a few already since I have been in Matilda's company.'

On seeing the expression of dismay on the detectives' faces, Georgina added, 'But of course we wouldn't do that, we're law-abiding citizens.'

'Yes,' Matilda agreed. 'Law-abiding.'

'Well, that's a relief,' Harry said with a chuckle.

'I'll sleep better in my bed tonight,' Thomas concurred.

'But you are not forgiven that easily, Thomas. I suffered numerous agonies last night, as did Detective Dart, I am sure,' Matilda scolded him. 'Despite Mrs Lawson suggesting I need to experience more of life, I would not like to experience that again too soon, thank you very much. You were almost the death of me.'

'Understood,' he said, saddened by the distress he had caused her. Thomas raised Matilda's hand to his lips again, not caring if Harry or Georgina witnessed the display of affection that he believed he owed her. The very thought of never seeing Matilda again was too much in his present condition, and feeling unwell, he released her hand and backed towards his desk to lean upon it.

'Should you be here?' Matilda asked.

'No,' Harry answered, and Thomas rolled his eyes.

'Speaking of Mrs Lawson, we have just come from the *Women's Journal* office, Detectives, with a request,' Georgina said and nodded at her new friend, Matilda, to continue.

'We are on deadline, and we thought we might try for a story exclusive to the *Women's Journal*,' Matilda added.

'Ah, well, no doubt you deserve it, just for putting up with Thomas,' Harry teased. 'I have not yet finished berating him, but I have plenty of time to continue that.'

Thomas looked embarrassed in front of the ladies and cleared his throat.

'I am sure I *deserve* Harry's censure,' he said uncharacteristically humble, and made Harry chuckle. 'But if my esteemed partner agrees, I too, think you deserve a lead given all the help you gave us with this case, we were just discussing it.'

'Really?' Matilda looked surprised. 'Well, that was unexpected. Mrs Lawson is holding the front page of the journal for me, but we have no time to waste. After that, the dailies will get the story first and we don't want that.'

'Absolutely not,' Harry agreed, teasing them.

'Besides, Georgina's drawings are amazing, and she will need to illustrate you both,' Matilda added.

'I can't wait to see that,' Harry said enthusiastically. 'I know I've got a few years on Thomas, but make me handsome, won't you Miss Urry?'

'It would be impossible not to, Detective Dart,' she said with a smile of affection for the mature, fine-looking, and kind detective. His salt-and-pepper hair and trim figure made him most distinguished. 'While you provide Matilda an audience and with your consent, I shall quickly illustrate both of you!' Georgina said, opening her pad and preparing.

'Of course,' Harry said, and looked to Thomas to begin his story.

'The case has not been concluded yet, not until we make an arrest,' Thomas said, 'but we know what was going on now.'

Harry looked surprised. He had not yet managed to get the full story from Thomas before the ladies interrupted. 'Let's hear it then,' he said. 'But it might not all be for publication,' he warned, and Matilda nodded her understanding.

Thomas winced, his hand involuntarily going to the back of his head from where the ache emanated. He joined the small party around his office table and took a seat.

'I have been trying to piece it all together in the correct order it happened,' Thomas began and told of what he had discovered and what Dr O'Shea had admitted to him when he had Thomas restrained and of no threat. Matilda hurriedly took notes, scratching out parts the detectives did not want her to reveal and checking names included in her story.

After hearing the astonishing story of Dr O'Shea accepting payment to kill his patients, Harry went back to the start. 'But how did he restrain you in the first place?'

Thomas rubbed the back of his head. 'A blow from behind felled me. I only sensed someone there at the last moment, and no, I didn't see their face, but they were dressed in white… it was an orderly.'

Harry nodded and looked away, thinking. 'So, the doctor had help. Do you remember anything about the orderly, Thomas? Think… a scent, a marking…'

'An accent,' Thomas said. 'He said a few words with an accent. German, I believe.'

'Is that so,' Harry said.

'Could it be our friend who helped us?' Georgina asked.

'Mr Derichs, Nikolaus,' Matilda said, recalling his name. 'He immediately knew where to go to find you, Thomas, but why would he lead us to you if he was complicit?'

The party rose as Harry said, 'I hope you have enough of the case, ladies, to make your story with Dr O'Shea as your villain?'

'Indeed we do, thank you both,' Matilda said with a glance at Georgina's wonderful illustrations.

Harry turned to Thomas. 'Since you are not going home, Thomas, we have work to do at the asylum. Let's finish this case once and for all.'

Women's Journal
Tuesday, 31 July 1888
Fortnightly edition Vol.1, No.20.
Price, 3d.

The murderous doctor at the asylum

An exclusive breakthrough in one of the city's most pitiful crimes. Report by Matilda Hayward. Illustrations by Georgina Urry.

--oOo--

The pitiful residents of the Asylum for the Insane at Wacol expect our sympathy and care, but this melancholy story is one of exploitation and betrayal with many victims.

Mrs Hilda Rodgers fought for her freedom. Wrongly committed by her husband, she was awarded her release when her son, Silas, came of age and could sign his mother out. A jury agreed Mrs Rodgers was sane and should not have been locked away. This made her death — a fall from the Victoria Bridge — that much more tragic. But it now seems her death was not suicide.

Her husband, Mr Raymond Rodgers was involved and then himself murdered but a week after her death. Detectives have connected the two fatal incidents.

Not long after the death of Mrs Hilda Rodgers, Mr Finch Turner's body was found in the burned remains of the recently destroyed Exhibition Building. He too was a former asylum resident but destitute and estranged from his wife, was living on the streets. The city's coroner, Dr Patrick Nevins, was able to determine that Mr Turner fell to his death before the fire.

Asylum resident, Mrs Meredith Martineau attempted to fly - to launch herself from the third-floor window and feel herself in flight, but she was pulled back before tragedy struck.

Mrs Birdie Sullivan, another asylum patient, was told she could fly. Her childlike paintings showed her emotional preparation for her flight, but she was too frightened to try. Both ladies are alive, but Mr Percy Sullivan took flight from an asylum window only last week and met his death.

At the heart of all this confusion

and loss is one man appointed to care for the residents of the asylum, Dr Stephen O'Shea.

Our city's finest detectives revealed the shocking truth - Dr O'Shea had accepted payments from estranged spouses of the asylum residents in return for ensuring as natural-seeming a death as possible commensurate with their conditions. The partners, then widowed, would claim on the life insurance or move on and remarry as was their wont.

How long this practice has been going on is yet to be determined, but in all deaths, excluding Mr Rodgers, the partners have benefited and it appears so has Dr O'Shea.

How did this come to the attention of our police force? According to Detective Thomas Ashdown and Detective Harry Dart, a clue indicated there was mischief afoot.

'At the death scene of Mr Raymond Rodgers, a bottle of medicine was found that was not prescribed to Mr Rodgers,' Detective Ashdown said. 'We traced this back to the asylum and found someone had recently administered the contents to Mrs Hilda Rodgers.'

Detective Dart continued the story: 'Unbeknown to her sons, Mrs Rodgers had been in pain and administered laudanum, which she quickly became addicted to as a painkiller. This brought upon her euphoria followed by terrible lows. With the encouragement of Dr O'Shea, Mrs Rodgers either believed that she could fly and was ready for flight or felt the despair so desperately from her low, that to jump was her only option of salvation.'

However, Mr Rodgers was not content with the manner of his estranged wife's death as he deemed it too public; he planned it to take place when Mrs Rodgers was still in residence at the asylum.

Dr Victor McQuade of the asylum — a subordinate of Dr O'Shea — confirmed for the Women's Journal that had Mrs Rodgers fallen to her death at the asylum, it would have been seen as in character with her assumed state of neurosis and not have attracted the police's attention.

When Dr O'Shea paid a visit to Mr Rodgers to collect his fee for the death of Mrs Rodgers, he was denied it, and the men argued.

'Finding a nearby rock, Dr O'Shea brutally struck Mr Rodgers,' Detective Dart informed the Women's Journal, 'the blow causing Mr Rodgers' death. The bottle of medicine fell from Dr O'Shea's pocket and was left at the scene.'

As a result, the detectives began looking more closely at the recent rate of deaths by falling and their connection to the asylum and laudanum.

'It had become a very viable business for Dr O'Shea,' Detective Ashdown said.

One can only imagine the anguish for a husband or wife to have their spouse committed to an asylum – unable to move forward with their life, not sure if they will ever resume their lives together. But those anguished by such circumstances surely would not wish their partner to be driven to fall from a great height due to fear or desperation.

By taking upon the role of the creator who gives and takes life, Dr O'Shea will now find himself behind the walls

of an asylum too, but in the form of a
prison.

*****

Matilda read and re-read her story and finally satisfied, gave
it to the Deputy Editor, Betty. Tonight, it would be printed
and tomorrow, it would be in the hands of readers.

Chapter 36

Thomas inhaled sharply as he caught sight of the asylum from the hansom cab he shared with Detective Dart. He didn't feel like himself just yet. He was embarrassed by needing assistance, by lying vulnerable in front of friends, family and strangers – especially Matilda – and he was feeling flat, thirsty and a little shaky. The sight of the asylum did not help.

'Are you all right, Thom?' Harry asked, studying his partner.

He nodded and swallowed, not trusting his voice.

'You need not do this. I can get a constable to attend with me,' Harry offered.

'No. I need to do this. I am up to the task, Harry. Let me,' Thomas said most assuredly. He ran a hand across his mouth, steeling himself. He felt Harry studying him and did not want to give the impression of weakness.

The hansom pulled up, and the men alighted.

The first person to accost them on arrival was Matron Gormley, on guard at the reception desk.

'Detectives,' she said, rising from her desk at reception. 'I hear you had quite an adventure,' she said to Thomas. 'We have procedures for safety which if followed should not result in harm to visitors.'

Thomas snapped back, 'One would think being escorted by one of your doctors would ensure my safety. But of course, if you had checked your visitor register, you would have noticed I did not sign out. Is the book for display or procedure?'

The matron's lips thinned, and she swallowed. 'What can I do for you today, gentlemen? Dr Hayward is on today if you wish to speak with him.'

Harry placed a hand on Thomas's arm and stepped in.

'No, thank you. We do not need to see Dr Hayward just yet. Matron, have you seen Dr O'Shea this morning?'

'He has not come in,' she said. 'But he also does house visits with potential and former patients if required, so his attendance can vary. Although…' she hesitated, 'he is usually here to do the morning rounds and handover.'

Neither of the detectives was surprised that Dr O'Shea had not shown his face if someone got word to him of Thomas's release. But who might have told him or did he not know yet and was genuinely late, leaving his prisoner locked below in the bowels of the hospital, knowing he was going nowhere?

'Can you tell me how many of your orderlies speak with an accent, specifically German?' Harry asked.

The matron thought for a few moments and then answered.

'Three I believe. Two are on shift today; one is on the night shift.'

'To the best of your knowledge, do any of these orderlies work closely with Dr O'Shea?' Harry asked.

'The young lad, Nikolaus Derichs. Dr O'Shea likes to take the younger staff under his wing. He's always been very personable and a wonderful trainer,' she said, flattering the doctor. Thomas wondered if she knew the full story about what happened to him or was simply devoted to Dr O'Shea, regardless of what he was capable of doing.

'Where might we find Mr Derichs?' Thomas asked impatiently.

'Nikolaus Derichs is rostered on the men's wing this morning, the first floor,' she said and pointed in the general direction.

Harry thanked her and the two men strode off, out the front door and over to the first-floor wing. Thomas stopped and Harry, not realising, walked on a few steps before looking back.

Thomas was leaning over slightly, a hand in his pocket, the other on his hips, his eyes closed. 'Just give me a minute, Harry.'

'You need to go—'

Thomas cut him off. 'Please, no lecture. Just one minute,' he said, waiting for nausea to pass. Harry stood beside him until Thomas opened his eyes, straightened, and with a nod, they went on.

Nikolaus Derichs was on his break when they arrived, sitting smoking in the garden outside the building. His eyes widened at the sight of the detectives, and he stood as they came towards him.

'A word if we may?' Harry asked and indicated for Nikolaus to take a seat again. Harry stood and Thomas lowered himself onto the bench at the other end from Nikolaus, pleased to sit for a moment.

'How are you feeling today, Detective?' Nikolaus asked with what appeared to be genuine concern.

'Better than last night,' Thomas answered.

'How did you know exactly where to find the detective last night?' Harry asked.

Thomas interrupted before Nikolaus spoke. 'We've been told by the matron that you work closely with Dr O'Shea, so the truth, please. I am short on patience and energy.'

'But of course,' Nikolaus answered, looking most affronted that he would say anything but the truth. He stretched to full height – a handsome, tall, young blond man who seemed to have no fear of the detectives. 'I am new and have very little choice who I work with, I do as I am told. I knew Dr O'Shea had his workrooms down on the lower floors of the unused wing.'

'Did you hit me yesterday afternoon?' Thomas asked.

'Yes,' he said, and both of the detectives' eyes widened. They rarely heard the truth, not on the first count anyway. 'I am sorry,' Nikolaus said. 'Dr O'Shea told me to inject you, but I… well, I was running late and then I left it upstairs, so I hit you.'

'You knew it was a detective that you were hitting?' Harry asked.

'Of course not.' Nikolaus Derichs shook his head in the negative. 'Dr O'Shea told me he was bringing a patient down to his rooms and the patient was delusional. He said the patient thought he was a banker coming to see some rooms, and we had to sedate him at the request of his family.'

The two detectives exchanged looks.

Nikolaus continued. 'When Miss Hayward and Miss Urry arrived looking for you, I knew straight away he had lied to me, and that it was you tied down in his rooms. I saw you once before, on the grounds, but I could not see you very well yesterday in the dark corridor and did not recognise you.'

'And you came from behind me,' Thomas recalled. 'Have you seen Dr O'Shea today?'

'Yes.'

Both men were startled.

'Here? At the asylum?' Harry asked.

'Yes.'

'The matron said otherwise.' Thomas's eyes narrowed… was she in on the ruse too? He rose, keen to entrap Dr O'Shea while he was on the premises.

'She may not have seen him. There is a private entrance,' Nikolaus offered. 'He is here now. He came and asked me where you were, and I said I didn't know.' Nikolaus looked from Thomas to Harry and back. 'It was not a lie; I didn't know where you were this morning. Am I going to be charged? I don't want to shame my family.'

Harry looked to Thomas to answer, it was after all his injury to bear.

Thomas shook his head. 'No, I can see you did your best under duress and Dr O'Shea deceived you.'

Nikolaus exhaled and ran his palms over his white pants, wiping them.

'Thank you,' he said. 'I assure you that I am a principled person. I work hard and am honest. Thank you,' he said again.

'Then help us find Dr O'Shea with haste. Can you escort us back to Dr O'Shea's underground rooms now?' Thomas asked with urgency.

'I can do better than that. Many patients are the eyes and ears of this place; they pride themselves on knowing what is going on.' Nikolaus stood and called out to several other orderlies to assist him momentarily, as they passed by with small groups of patients on their way to workshops or the gardens.

The two orderlies told their patients to wait as Nikolaus approached them and explained what they needed. One of the senior orderlies nodded, then clapped his hands loudly. He yelled, 'Listen up everyone, we need your help. Dr O'Shea has been very bad, and we need to find him. Don't touch him, just help us find him for these two detectives. Starting now,' he said as though it was a race.

Nikolaus thanked him and returned to the detectives. Thomas watched as the patients looked at each other and around the grounds as if Dr O'Shea might pop out of the shrubbery. Several hurried off.

'They'll spread the word,' Nikolaus said. 'Let us go, I'll take you to the rooms now.'

They followed the young, handsome man who was showing his leadership qualities, straight back into the dark, damp cells of the asylum.

Chapter 37

Through the doorway of the *Women's Journal* office came a young man bearing a gift. He was dressed in the uniform of a delivery man with a small hat. The receptionist gasped on seeing the gift, and standing, she pointed to the lady recipient. All eyes turned enviously, and the young man smiled as he carried the two dozen red roses – at the peak of blooming – down the centre of the room. There were sighs of disappointment from the ladies he passed, smiles of appreciation from those who knew the roses were not for them but remembered when they might have been, and great hope on the faces of the ladies who dreamed.

He turned at the halfway mark of the room and headed towards the ladies by the window, where the light was best for those who illustrated.

'Miss Georgina Urry?' he asked of the three ladies seated.

Georgina gasped. 'Goodness me, that's me! Are they for me?'

She stood looking far from confident – not in her own name, that much she knew – but thinking the young man might have made a mistake.

He smiled. 'They are, Miss Urry,' he said, and carefully handed Georgina the enormous bouquet of perfect red roses.

'Oh my, thank you,' she said, placing them carefully on the table behind her, in full advantage of everyone's sight. The nearby ladies gathered around to smell and admire them as the young man departed, having enjoyed his moment of attention, which was now transferred to the roses.

Matilda clapped her hands, excited, and Georgina glanced at her, waving the card. Georgina pulled it from its envelope.

'Can you tell us or is it too private?' Alice squealed, 'please tell us!' The ladies laughed around her.

Georgina read the message, smiled, and closed her eyes, pressing the card against her heart. She opened her eyes again; they were not misty – she was far too practical for that even though this was the first time she had received roses from a potential suitor.

'It reads,' she said, dragging out the suspense:

*'A rose for every hour I have thought of you since yesterday.
My deepest affection, Elijah.'*

There were moans around her, and several ladies touched their hearts. Matilda came to Georgina's side and hugged her, as did Alice.

'I am so happy,' Matilda said, blinking back tears.

'Not as happy as I am. Your dear, sweet brother,' Georgina said with a sigh.

'Have you any more brothers?' Ursula Woodfield, one of the young typewriter operators, asked, which engaged more laughing.

'I have four, but I think they might all be taken now.' Matilda smiled. 'Darling Elijah,' she said with a smile, looking at the roses and thinking of the dozen at home from her Thomas.

'I think he is smitten,' Alice agreed, and Georgina laughed.

As the girls returned to their desks, but before she could depart, Georgina reached for Matilda's hands and said so that only she could hear, 'I am grateful for all the kindness you have shown me, Matilda.'

'Nonsense,' Matilda said, 'we are firm friends.'

'Yes, and for that, I am grateful. While I might appear gregarious, I am not always comfortable in the company of people, and I have been feeling quite homesick. You have made me feel welcome and not once have you made me feel awkward, despite what my size and manners might dictate.'

'Georgina, you are too hard on yourself,' Matilda said. 'You are a most handsome, clever and interesting woman, and after our last adventure, definitely a risk taker too!' Georgina laughed and Matilda added, 'The pleasure of your company has been mine.'

Georgina nodded her grateful thanks and looked again at the roses. 'I wish my mother could see these roses. She fears I am going to end up a spinster talking to the cows on our farm,' she said with a chuckle. 'I have never seen anything so beautiful.'

'Apparently, my brother feels the same,' Matilda said with a grin.

'It's empty!' Harry exclaimed, turning in a circle as he took in all the bare shelves of the room that was once full of bottles.

'How can that be?' Nikolaus asked, and looked back out into the hallway, counting doorways to ensure he had the right room.

Thomas shook his head with frustration. 'Dr O'Shea has cleared out all his potions, but that must have taken some time. He can't have got far.'

'You mentioned there is another entrance or exit that avoids coming by the matron and reception?' Harry asked.

'Yes, it comes out in the garden. Follow me,' Nikolaus said, carrying the lamp through the area that was too dark even of a daytime not to have some form of lighting.

'Makes sense,' Thomas said. 'If you were sneaking in wilful patients after hours, you might not want to come via the traditional route.'

Harry followed at the rear, believing Thomas to be too jittery after the blow to his head to be left vulnerable in the corridors of the asylum. At least there was safety in numbers.

'It's not far,' Nikolaus assured them after a few more turns.

'Stop,' Thomas ordered, and the group froze. 'Hear that? Someone is above us.'

The group heard fast footfalls echoing in the empty corridor above their heads.

'That is the way we are going, hurry,' Nikolaus said and started at a fast pace, the men catching up to the light bobbing ahead. At the end, they tore up a set of stairs and winced as a door at the other end of the corridor was ajar, their eyes adjusting to the brightness.

'He had to go through there,' Nikolaus said, continuing in pursuit.

Before the three men had broken out into the light and garden, they heard yelling. Nikolaus could not move fast enough for them now. Breaking clear into the garden, the detectives stopped suddenly at the sight in front of them.

A circle had been formed. In the middle stood the doctor, a large carry bag by his feet, his hands up in supplication. He smiled and jested, using the charm that had won him much popularity until now. Around him, half a dozen patients had formed a circle and two orderlies stood nearby.

'Bad man,' one patient kept saying and several others nodded.

'Now, now, that is just silly, isn't it?' Dr O'Shea was saying as he called the patients by name and attempt to relax them. 'How are you today, Reginald? And Theodore, let's hasten to your garden work then, shall we?'

His eyes widened as he saw the sight of Nikolaus and the two detectives.

Harry and Thomas moved closer, and Harry said to the group, 'Thank you all for your assistance. Your duty has been done and we are very grateful.'

Smiles flickered among the men, and some stood taller, their chests puffed.

'I suggest you come with us now, Dr O'Shea,' Thomas said.

The bravado fell from the doctor's face, and he looked around. There was nowhere to run; his shoulders slumped, and he appeared resigned to his fate.

'Is there a room in which we can detain Dr O'Shea securely until our constables arrive?' Harry asked.

'There are plenty of rooms for that purpose,' Nikolaus said.

'You should be grateful we don't put you in the basement where you restrained me,' Thomas muttered. He looked up to see Elijah and Nurse Hopkins watching the drama unfold from the third level of the female ward. He raised his hand in thanks.

Several of the orderlies returned to their duties with their patients, while one of them along with Nikolaus and the two detectives, escorted Dr O'Shea to be locked up. For the first time in all his years of practice, Dr O'Shea would feel what it was like for his patients to lose their independence.

Departing some time after, Harry exhaled with relief. 'We've got our man, Thom. Justice has been done.'

'We have, but I will not rest until I get all those files from the asylum – the deaths during Dr O'Shea's tenure. Let's see how many died from falls and how many had insurance policies and willing spouses.'

'I am hoping Dr O'Shea has kept a record… a little black book maybe, of all the fees he took against associated names.

That will make it easier to follow up the partners who were prepared to pay for the deaths of their incarcerated,' Harry said. 'That may take some time, but at least the man in question has now been caught.'

'With no chance of being let off regardless of what else we uncover,' Thomas said with relief.

Harry nodded. 'Agreed. Let us get a hansom cab. Best you sit at a desk for the rest of the day,' he suggested.

Thomas exhaled. 'Today, I will not argue with you on that front.'

'Goodness, another win for me,' Harry said, and Thomas laughed.

Harry looked at his protégé with humour and affection. Their record of solved cases continued to be second to none, and Thomas, well and safe, would return to the arms of his beloved this evening.

Chapter 38

After the excitement of the rose delivery had died down at the *Women's Journal*, there was much excitement again when the latest edition, straight from the press, was delivered. There was nothing like the thrill of seeing the finished product and a story or illustration come to life with a name in print.

Mrs Lawson came out of her office to take delivery and, taking the first issue, invited the ladies to secure their copies. Together, they leafed through it, admiring the stories and illustrations, the layout and quality.

'Well done, ladies, another excellent issue,' Mrs Lawson said, thanking her employees before returning to her office with the deputy editor, Betty, to review it.

Matilda was nervous and excited to see her work come to life in print, knowing too, that there was no opportunity to amend the content – this was the edition that everyone would read, including Aunt Audrey. She admired Georgina's illustrations and read her own story one more time with pride, feeling delighted at seeing her name in print beside the article.

Well pleased, she glanced at the personal columns and advertisements, which were always intriguing. Then Matilda froze. She looked up to find ladies smiling and stealing looks at her.

She looked again and read the small advertisement titled:
'A gentleman caller.'

The copy read:

*'Mr T. Ashdown would like the pleasure of calling on
Miss M. Hayward this Sunday
with the intention of serious business.'*

Matilda laughed and looked up. Questions were asked and the ladies congratulated her on what they understood the notice to mean. She smiled with delight, her heart racing with excitement.

'I did challenge him to make my proposal memorable,' she said.

'Oh, he has done very well,' Alice said and clapped her hands with delight. 'How clever to support the very place you work, and to be so cloak and dagger – you do love a mystery.'

'It is you to a T,' Georgina called from across the room.

'What an exciting day,' Betty said on her way back to her desk from Mrs Lawson's office. 'Roses, mystery advertisements, a new edition. I think I may need a cup of tea and possibly a biscuit.'

'Morning tea for all, then?' Mrs Lawson said, coming out of her office and hearing Betty's comments. Tea, cake and biscuits were served and for the next forty-five minutes, the ladies socialised and celebrated in the spirit of sisterhood.

*****

Hilda Rodgers's son, Silas, bowed his fair head as the detectives delivered the news to him and his brothers.

'I am sorry, lads,' Harry said, 'but I hope it brings you some comfort to know that your mother did not willingly take her own life. She was under the influence of two very dominant men and a terrible drug.'

'So even though he did not do it with his own hand, our father killed our mother,' Claude, the second eldest brother, said, anger riding his voice.

'Yes, and Dr O'Shea will be punished, though unfortunately, your father will not.'

'Not on this earth anyway,' Claude said. He crossed his arms over his chest, the strongest of all the boys. 'What was he prepared to pay? What was Mum's life worth?'

'We don't know that yet,' Thomas answered truthfully. 'But we've requisitioned all Dr O'Shea's effects and we'll be charging all partners that have paid for the removal of their husbands or wives.'

The youngest lad, Jesse turned away to hide his emotions, and Silas moved to him, cuffing an arm around him in an embrace.

'What now for you lads?' Harry asked. 'You are fine young men; your mother would want you to make the best of your lives.'

'And you'll have the funds to do so,' Thomas added.

Silas nodded and smiled at his brothers. 'We've put in an offer to buy these premises. We're going to call if the *Baking Brothers*.'

Harry laughed. 'Excellent. And shall you continue to reside here?'

'For a while,' Claude answered.

'You wouldn't consider moving home?' Thomas asked.

All three boys declined the idea.

'We have very few happy memories there,' Silas said. 'I am sorry that the staff will need to find new positions, but that can't be helped. We will sell it and live here until each of my brothers is ready to buy his own place and leave.'

The two brothers smiled.

'Jesse has his eye on a young lady already,' Silas teased his young brother, who reddened.

'Well, we'll be sure to drop in if we're in the area,' Harry said cordially.

Thomas never would. He did not like to revisit old crimes and victims, but he appreciated the sentiment.

The bell rang, and the boys straightened as a couple of ladies entered. Jesse wiped his face and went to serve them.

'We've got some buns straight out of the oven. I'll pack a few for you,' Silas said. 'It is close to lunchtime.'

'We wouldn't say no to that, thank you,' Harry said.

Thomas inhaled. 'Starving,' he muttered as the clock neared twelve. 'Shall we eat on the way?'

Harry nodded. 'Let's grab a couple of constables and go make an arrest.'

*****

Thomas knocked on the door of a comfortable establishment outside of the city borders and stood back. Behind him, Harry and two constables waited. The curtain moved and then the door was opened by a large woman wearing a scowl.

Harry was about to remove his hat when she asked, 'What would you be wanting then?' He left it on.

'Mrs Finch Turner?' Thomas asked.

'Yes. Enid Turner. My husband's not here; he's dead,' she said.

'We are aware of that Mrs Turner and we are aware of your part in his death,' Thomas said, studying her.

She scoffed. 'His demise is entirely his fault. He was a drunkard, a gambler, and even the asylum rejected him given there was nothing wrong with him except his wilfulness.'

'So, you threw him out on the mercy of the streets?' Harry asked.

'I threw him out a lot of times, but he always came back. It's his fault he got caught in that fire at the Exhibition Building. He was sleeping it off there and happened to be in the wrong place at the wrong time. Just as I was when he first courted me,' she said with a smirk.

'Except, Mrs Turner, we know from the coroner's findings that your husband did not die from the fire. He died from a fall because he believed he could fly,' Thomas said, never taking his eyes off her face as he studied her reactions.

She laughed. 'What did I tell you? They should have kept him at the asylum.'

'Perhaps you will not be as amused to know that we spoke with Dr O'Shea from the asylum.'

Her countenance changed, and then she steeled herself.

Thomas could imagine her inventing lies as she waited for his next announcement.

'We know you paid a sum of money to Dr O'Shea to rid yourself of your husband,' Thomas said.

'And that you took out a life insurance policy on his life only three months prior,' Harry added.

She started to speak, then instead tried to slam the door closed.

Harry wedged himself in the doorway, pushing it open. 'Mrs Enid Turner, we are arresting you for being complicit in the murder of your husband…'

Thomas nodded to the constables who came forward to restrain Mrs Turner and take her to the jail cells.

'I wish we had the pleasure of seeing Meredith's husband arrested,' Thomas said.

'As do I,' Harry agreed, 'and I hope the English bobbies can find Earl Martineau. At least time is on our side… Meredith is still alive, and he will not know yet that the man he paid the bribe to – Dr O'Shea – has been arrested.'

As the constables led Mrs Turner down the path, Thomas entered the house. There was no sign of anyone else, person or pet. Hung on the wall over the fireplace was a large photo of the happily married couple. He turned to leave and catch up with Harry outside, closing the door behind him.

Chapter 39

It was a festive and happy lunch on Sunday after church with much to celebrate. Thomas was safe and well, the twins – Gideon and Elijah – had each lost their hearts and secured love, and Amos and Minnie had some news of their own. In each pocket of the Hayward drawing and dining rooms were small groups of family talking animatedly.

The Hayward patriarch and, by default, the matriarch – his sister, Audrey – spoke in the entrance hall where Audrey had just arrived.

'Goodness, dear brother, you may need to extend the dining room once the grandchildren come along,' Aunt Audrey said, studying the Hayward household and finding so many young people in attendance.

Audrey thanked Harriet, who took her coat and hat, and Mr Hayward nodded his head in agreement.

'Perhaps I'd best get to work updating the conservatory to house us all for lunch. It could be quite lovely amidst the garden,' he said, thrilled at the prospect. 'How Jane would have loved to see her children so happy.' He sighed, thinking of his beloved wife, long gone now.

Audrey touched his arm. 'Indeed, a fine tribute to your efforts, brother. Let us remember Jane, but not be maudlin today.'

'I could not agree more,' he said.

'Besides, your happiness is on my list too,' Audrey said. 'I have met a lovely widow – a most attractive woman in her bloom, conservative and eloquent, I think you might be suited…'

In another corner, Daniel and Alice were introduced to Miss Lily Chappell, on the arm of the youngest family member, Gideon. Matilda joined them as her beau, Thomas, did not attend church and had not yet arrived but was expected any moment.

'Goodness what an enormous family,' Lily said, her eyes wide as she took in the group.

'It is, more so now that my brothers have all partnered and about time,' Matilda said with a teasing look at Daniel and Gideon in her company.

'I'm delighted to be welcomed into the family,' Alice said on Daniel's arm, and he smiled down at her with genuine affection.

Matilda noted he was quite subdued around Alice, as though in awe of her presence and on his best behaviour. She wondered how long that would last, and turned her attention to Lily as the group chatted. Lily was beautiful, doll-like, with her heart-shaped face, large expressive eyes and brunette curls. She appeared to Matilda to be too taken up with her own presence to remember her date beside her – Gideon – but Matilda determined that was probably nerves on Lily's part, having to meet so many in surroundings that were unfamiliar to her. Besides, it did not matter if Lily Chappell was an affected young lady as long as she adored and cared for Gideon, Matilda thought.

'I have met your brother, Elijah,' Lily said, holding court, 'but then I met his twin brother who is so handsome,' she teased, holding Gideon's arm.

'So very handsome,' Gideon agreed with a wink to Matilda to defy him.

'And much more suited to you, I imagine, Miss Chappell,' Matilda said. 'Gideon is so energetic we must occupy him every moment of the day and no doubt you will do a fine job of that task.'

'Do you work?' Alice asked Gideon's date.

'Goodness, no!' Lily exclaimed, and Matilda had to disguise her spontaneous laugh as a cough.

Daniel was not so tactful. 'Miss Chappell, you are among the suffragettes now… Alice and Matilda both write for the *Women's Journal*, and you will meet Elijah's lady today, she is an illustrator for the publication,' Daniel said.

'Elijah has a lady friend?' Lily replied, ignoring all else.

And as if on cue, Elijah entered with Miss Georgina Urry on his arm. Only Thomas remained to arrive, and he was cutting it terribly fine, Matilda thought. But she knew Thomas would not risk the wrath of Cook if it could be helped, even if Cook had a soft spot for him and accepted his work excuses for being late when she accepted nobody else's.

Matilda saw Lily's eyes widen as she studied Georgina. Compared to Lily, Georgina was easily a foot or so taller, wider, and hardly dressed in the latest fashions, even though she could easily afford them.

'Goodness, is that Elijah's date?' she said and gave a small laugh. She looked up at Gideon.

Gideon's loyalty to his twin was unshakable. 'Elijah has lost his heart to Miss Urry, I believe,' he said. 'She is a country lass and I hear most talented and charming.'

'Very talented, a fine illustrator in fact,' Alice added, 'like my Daniel,' she teased, and he brought her hand to his lips.

'A country girl, well that explains her manner,' Lily said, noting the lack of polish that had been lacquered upon her own upbringing.

'She is one of our dearest friends,' Matilda added to be sure this was known, 'is she not, Alice?'

'Oh indeed, and such fun.' Desiring to keep the peace, Alice added, 'Have you met Minnie?' Alice raised her eyebrows at Gideon, who understood and stepped up.

'Yes, introductions are in order, excuse us,' he said, slipping away with Miss Chappell.

'This will be fun, won't it?' Daniel muttered, and the ladies smiled. 'Two ladies who don't believe in working, three ambitious ladies who do, and a couple – Miss Urry and Matilda – who could use a month at finishing school,' he said with a glance at Matilda and laughed at her reaction.

After playfully hitting his arm, she turned to Alice. 'You managed that beautifully, thank you.'

'I am one of three daughters… diplomacy, tact and sometimes bribery is required among we ladies,' Alice said with a knowing look.

Harriet announced lunch was served and as the family moved into the dining room, the front door opened, and Thomas rushed in.

Matilda grinned, and excusing herself from Daniel and Alice, hurried to meet him.

'Just in time, young man,' Aunt Audrey said, passing him with a smile.

'Aunt Audrey, Mr Hayward,' Thomas greeted them as he removed his hat and coat and thanked Harriet. He took Matilda's hand and kissed it. 'My apologies, station business, but all is under control again, I believe.'

'It is,' she agreed, 'all is well now you are here.' And, with her arm looped through his, they joined the family at lunch.

But it was the after-lunch walk where Thomas would put into place his plan… his proposal. He had forewarned Matilda with his advertisement and could not wait to hear her reply. Lunch could not finish quickly enough for him on this Sunday.

Unfortunately, he had made the mistake of telling his best friend, Daniel, of his intent to propose in the gardens on their walk.

Chapter 40

Mr Hayward agreed with his son, Daniel.

'It is a fine afternoon for a walk, and it seems a shame to break up our lovely party so early. Shall we all take a stroll then?'

If Thomas's look could have struck Daniel down, he would have melted to the ground then and there. The party, having survived lunch without too much contention given the variety of views present and sometimes heated debates, progressed outside to meander to the gardens. Even Aunt Audrey thought the idea a fine one and accepted Amos's arm – her favourite Hayward boy – while Mr Hayward escorted Minnie, delighting in her news that she was in the family way with his first grandchild.

While Alice engaged Georgina in conversation, Thomas pulled Daniel aside, annoyed at the size of the group that had trespassed on his plan.

'What the hell are you doing?' he hissed.

'Strolling. Oh, you mean… I assure you none of us will get in the way of your proposal, I'll make sure of it,' Daniel said with a glance back at his sister.

'I am taking her to the rose garden. It is in full bloom and there is a lovely bench there, as long as it is not already taken,' he said. 'Can you steer everyone away from there?'

'Consider it done. I'll herd the group elsewhere to ensure you are both alone,' Daniel teased him and received a less-than-pleased look from Thomas, who was now regretting mentioning his intent while caught up in nerves and the excitement of his plan.

Behind him, Miss Lily Chappell had now taken his place beside Matilda and was engaging her in conversation.

'I fear you might not think too highly of me, Matilda,' Lily was saying as they happily agreed to address each other more intimately.

Matilda looked surprised. 'Dear Lily, what would make you think that, especially as we barely know each other?'

'For two reasons. I fear I was flippant about your friend, Georgina, earlier at lunch, but you are correct. She is wonderful company.'

Matilda smiled at Lily and hooked arms with her, to Thomas's dismay. Could he just have one moment alone to perform the proposal he had been planning in his head for days? He patted his pocket to ensure the ring was still there and was satisfied feeling the small box waiting to be presented.

'I am so glad you think so too,' Matilda was saying. 'We will have fun, all of us ladies, I am sure of it. What on earth was the second reason?'

'That I have moved from one brother to the next,' she said and lowered her voice.

Matilda's eyes moved over Lily's doll-like face. Thomas wished they were on him alone. He hovered ahead slightly, waiting for his turn to move behind and steal Matilda away. He was half listening to the conversation beside him he was meant to be engaged in.

Lily continued in a low voice, 'I assure you I did indeed find your brother, Elijah, very handsome, but I had only met him a few times. But I felt an instant attraction to Gideon, and have great affection for him, already,' she said looking towards Gideon.

Matilda smiled. 'They are so very different of nature, one would not believe they are twins, except to look at them. I think you and Gideon are very suited.'

On hearing his name, he came to their side and, to Thomas's delight, steered Lily away to have her to himself. Thomas took the opportunity.

'Come, Matilda, I wish to show you something. We can catch up with the family later,' he said before anyone else interrupted them for a chat, which mind you, they had been having at lunch for the last few hours.

'Lead on,' she said, turning her lovely face to him.

Thomas did his best not to hurry her, for it was an afternoon stroll after all. Moments later, they had slipped into the rose garden away from the family's prying eyes, and to his great relief, no one was sitting on the bench.

He suggested they sit awhile and wiped the bench clean with his handkerchief. He accepted Matilda's thanks as she seated herself, and he beside her. They were alone.

*****

Of course, Matilda knew what was coming, she was just wondering when Thomas might deliver his proposal. He had all his preparation complete – her father's approval, the advertisement of intent placed in her magazine to make it memorable and special, and now, she was sure the moment had come.

She looked up at him as they sat, wide-eyed and attentive, and indeed keen. Thomas cleared his throat, subtly patted his pocket again, and was just about to drop beside her on one knee when Daniel and Alice appeared around the corner.

Matilda noticed Daniel gave Thomas an apologetic look.

'I wanted to see the roses,' Alice said and looked delighted to find so many in bloom. She sniffed a beautiful white one nearby. 'My mother has such lovely rose gardens.'

'They are beautiful, and the winter is the best time for them in our Brisbane climate,' Matilda agreed, admiring the pink ones in full bloom beside her.

Matilda suppressed a smile as she saw the glare Thomas was giving Daniel.

'I must show you the ducks, Alice,' Daniel said. 'I could have sworn I saw some ducklings the other day.'

'It is too early, surely, but let us go. I'd love to see the ducklings,' Alice agreed and with enthusiasm, they walked past, disappearing from the garden.

Thomas sighed, bracing himself again for action, when they heard a cough behind them and around the edge of the shrubbery came Elijah and Georgina.

'You are right, Elijah, they are splendid,' Georgina said, upon seeing the roses.

Matilda greeted them and heard Thomas groan and shuffle with annoyance beside her. She looked at him with surprise, as if she could not imagine why he was annoyed to see her dear brother and friend.

'Have you been in the gardens before now?' Elijah asked Georgina.

'No, not since arriving in the city. I am so pleased to be outdoors at any time, but the gardens are exceptionally beautiful. I must come in and draw some time. Perhaps you could find something medical to do and accompany me? An operation perhaps?' she joked.

He laughed. 'I'll bring a medical journal and read. It will be less messy.'

'There is a fine drinking fountain that should be seen,' Thomas suggested, cutting into their conversation, and gave Matilda a small shrug when she looked at him with surprise.

'Let's investigate,' Elijah said, and with a nod to Matilda and Thomas, they continued on their way.

Thomas sighed and Matilda smiled as she turned to him. 'I too would like to see the drinking fountain. I didn't know you had such an interest in it.'

'I don't. We can pass there later if you like,' he said, trying not to rush the afternoon or change the mood.

Thomas took another deep breath. Matilda could sense his nervousness; she had known him most of his life, after all.

'You seem short of breath, are you quite well?' she asked as if concerned for his health after his recent episode with laudanum.

'Thank you, I am quite well,' he answered, steeling himself.

And then Gideon and Lily appeared around the corner of the shrubbery. Thomas rose and threw his hands up in the air.

'For the love of God,' he said.

Behind them, hidden by the tall hedge, there was much laughter and soon all members of the family appeared. Matilda laughed at seeing them all and, ignoring the lot of them, Thomas gave in and dropped to one knee.

When Matilda turned back to set eyes on him, he was gone from the bench and, she found him kneeling beside her. She gasped, her eyes lit with excitement and happiness.

'Matilda, will you do me the great honour of being my wife?' he asked, looking at her only and ignoring everyone else. He could wait no longer and did not care if there were a thousand witnesses.

'Yes, yes definitely Thomas, I would love to be your wife,' she said, and he raised her hand to his lips and kissed it.

The family cheered and around them, there was much jubilation. Thomas rose and with Matilda, joined in the kissing and back-slapping.

'I shall never tell you anything in confidence again, Daniel,' Thomas said, despite not being angry.

Daniel laughed and so all could hear he added, 'You have annoyed us for years and now we are giving you our only sister. It is only fair there should be some payback.'

'Years and years,' Gideon agreed. 'You can't expect us not to all be involved – that would break tradition.'

'Indeed,' Thomas said with resignation, and Matilda held his hand with delight, not caring who saw their happiness.

Mr Hayward congratulated the pair. 'I assure you, Thom, Matilda dear, they coerced me into appearing,' he said with a wink.

'Is there a ring?' Aunt Audrey asked, ever the one for protocols.

'Yes,' Thomas said hurriedly reaching into his pocket. He brought out a small dark box and opened it. Inside on the red velvet sat a large and dramatic solitaire diamond in a gold setting. Around him, commentary broke out.

'Oh my,' Matilda said, her eyes wide.

'That is stunning,' Georgina said.

'Breathtaking,' Alice added.

'I've never seen a diamond so big,' Lily added.

Minnie looked at her ring and smiled at Amos. Thomas ignored the gallery and slipped it onto Matilda's finger.

'It is so beautiful and enormous,' Matilda said, holding her hand afar.

'There goes the house painting and six months' salary,' Daniel added.

'The best investment I will ever make,' Thomas said, enjoying the looks of affection from all the ladies, but especially Matilda.

Aunt Audrey took Matilda's hand to study the ring and then announced, 'Well, I must say, young man, that is the most handsome ring I have ever seen. Excellent cut, exquisite design, unique. Absolutely beautiful,' she declared.

'Yes,' Thomas said, looking at Matilda. 'Unique and beautiful.'

Daniel shook his head and Thomas, on seeing him, grinned at his best friend.

'I will remember this, Daniel,' he warned him, with a glance at Alice who giggled beside him.

After many congratulations, Mr Hayward announced, 'Harriet has champagne waiting at home. I suggest we all partake in a glass and leave the happy couple to have a moment to bask in their joy alone.'

'We'll save two glasses for you,' Alice said, squeezing Matilda's hand with excitement.

And soon they were alone again.

'That was not quite how I planned it,' Thomas said as they sat back on the bench.

'It was perfect,' Matilda said. 'Everyone I love was with us, and my husband to be beside me. Mrs Thomas Ashdown…' she said and added, 'Mrs Matilda Ashdown.'

'Mr and Mrs Ashdown,' Thomas added.

'Let us go and have some champagne. I need to show Harriet my beautiful engagement ring,' Matilda said with excitement.

'I cannot keep you from being in the moment's joy with our family and friends. But I will have my just reward,' he said and Matilda reddened slightly. It was not like her to be coy around Thomas, but she studied his eyes and then his lips as he leaned in for his first kiss on her lips.

The day was warm, the scent of roses filled the air and the young couple kissed in perfect happiness and love.

'Maybe we should stay longer,' she said, and he laughed.

'I love you, Matilda, I always have.'

'I love you, Thomas,' she said for the first time and gave him a small smile, her eyes saying everything that needed to be said.

Rising, he offered Matilda his arm. 'Come, let us return home.'

And then, from her small bag, she searched, finding it, and pulled out a dainty ring.

'What is that?' he asked as they walked towards the Hayward household.

'The ring you gave me when I was twelve and you promised to marry me,' she said, looking at the little band with a fake stone that would only fit on her smallest finger now.

'And you kept it, all this time?' He smiled, delighted.

'I was intending to keep you to your word,' she said.

He pulled her closer as they walked and added, 'Of course if I had known you still had that ring, there would have been no need to buy you the other.'

Matilda looked at him, playfully shocked, and he laughed.

'We are engaged!' she said as if it had just sunk in. 'Now, my fiancé, I wonder what our next adventure will be?'

'Well, I imagine you need to consider bridal gowns and venues…'

'Oh there's all that,' she agreed, cutting him off, 'but I was thinking of your next case and how I can help with a story!'

'Of course, how exciting,' he said in a droll voice, and Matilda laughed.

'Indeed.'

And they walked home together, arm in arm, ready to start their next chapter together.

THE END

Next, read on, as Matilda's adventures continue in '*The Mortician's Clue*'.

Also in the Miss Hayward and the Detective series:

Murder at the Freak Show
The Artist's Missing Muse
Mystery at the Asylum
The Mortician's Clue
Murder in Bridal Lane

Author's note:

While this is a book of fiction and the characters and situations have been created in my mind and musings, I have tried to be as historically accurate as possible to the events, locations and customs of 1888.

The comments Elijah shares with the boys about Dr O'Shea's radical views that 'much flesh-eating induced masturbation' were the considered thoughts of Australian asylum superintendent William Beattie Smith in 1903[1]. The Brisbane Exhibition Building did indeed burn down in 1888 and electric lightning had been experimented with at the time. Alice's reporting on the women's movement was based on the first International Women's Conference held in Washington, DC in 1888 with speakers and delegates from nine countries.

The characters of the ladies at the asylum were inspired by the writings of Helen Vellacott[2] (nee Fancourt McDonald) who was six years old when her family came to live at the Willowburn Mental Asylum in Toowoomba in 1918, or the Lunatic Asylum, as it was known. Her father was the resident doctor, Dr James Edward Fancourt McDonald. She wrote of the patients she met such as the dressmaker, the young indigenous woman who could make the animal prints with her hands, and a lady who spoke to the sky. She also wrote of the work ethic of the asylum. *My* ladies' characteristics were broadly drawn from Helen's remembrances but definitely not meant to represent the original ladies, their lives or struggles.

While the numbers I quoted of 350 male and 200 female patients in Elijah's workplace – the asylum – might sound like a lot, in some asylums, patient numbers were close to 800.

Nellie Bly is a real journalist who went undercover in a New York Insane Asylum in 1887, and wrote a series titled *Ten Days in a Mad-House*. Her style of reporting ushered in a new age of newspaper writing. Girl power!

Also in the *Miss Hayward and the Detective* series...

Murder at the Freak Show

Matilda Hayward is determined to have a career, after all, it is 1888! While reporting for the *Women's Journal* newspaper, Matilda is sent to cover the visiting 'Freak Show' and to interview Mrs Anna Tufton, a giantess. During the interview, the giantess slips a note to Matilda begging for her help to escape from the show she is forced to do by her husband. But when the giantess's husband is found murdered, the giantess is a likely suspect.

Matilda enlists her lawyer brother, Amos, to help prove the giantess is no killer and to free her from a life of exploitation. But a close family friend, Detective Thomas Ashdown – who has feelings for Matilda having known her since childhood – would prefer Matilda was nowhere near his murder case. There is mystery, danger, and love afoot!

*****

The Artist's Missing Muse

Miss Matilda Hayward admits she is no art critic but when she meets artist, Mr Marlon Dominey, and his beautiful muse, Miss Sapphire Reubens, she can appreciate beauty on and off the canvas. Her brother and art gallery manager, Gideon, is to exhibit Mr Dominey's latest collection and Matilda and Miss Alice Doran – her fellow writer for the *Women's Journal* – get a preview of the inspired work featuring his muse illuminated and immersed in water.

But when muse, Miss Reubens, can't be found, and two artists are found murdered and posed in the manner of their paintings, Matilda and her new beau, Detective Thomas Ashdown, fear the artwork might be a death portrait. There is mystery, passion and love afoot!

✶✶✶✶✶

The Mortician's Clue

Miss Matilda Hayward has been assigned her first book review for the *Women's Journal* newspaper and she is very much enjoying Mr Linton Turner's novel, *The Pyjama Girl Mystery*, until it comes to life. When a young lady is found murdered and left on the church steps dressed only in blue satin pyjamas – just like in the plot of the novel – the author immediately comes under suspicion. But no one can identify the victim.

Matilda's beau, Detective Thomas Ashdown, is on the case, and with his partner, Detective Harry Dart, they hire a talented mortician, Miss Phoebe Astin, to illustrate the deceased lady for identification purposes. After Matilda and her friend, Miss Georgina Urry, make Phoebe's acquaintance, the three ladies find themselves unwillingly caught in a battle of words and hearts between an author and a poet with deadly intent. There is secrecy, danger, and love afoot!

*****

References:

1 Wallis, Alexandra, Theses: Hysterical Women: Moral Treatment of Female Patients in the Fremantle Lunatic Asylum, 1858 – 1908, *The University of Notre Dame Australia*, 2020.
2 Vellacott, Helen, Some Memories of Willowburn, *Baillie Henderson Mental Health Museum*, 19 July 2010. Retrieved 15 April 2019 from URL: http://bailliemuseum.wikidot.com/willowburnmemories

About the Author:

After studying English Literature and Communications at universities in Queensland, Australia, and obtaining a Counselling Diploma, Helen Goltz has worked as a journalist, producer and marketer in print, TV, radio and public relations. She was born in Toowoomba and has made her home in Brisbane.

Visit her website at: www.helengoltz.com

Or Facebook at: www.facebook.com/HelenGoltz.Author

Follow on Twitter at: https://twitter.com/HelenGwriter

Sign-up for Helen's newsletter on her webiste to hear when the next *Miss Hayward and the Detective* adventure is released!